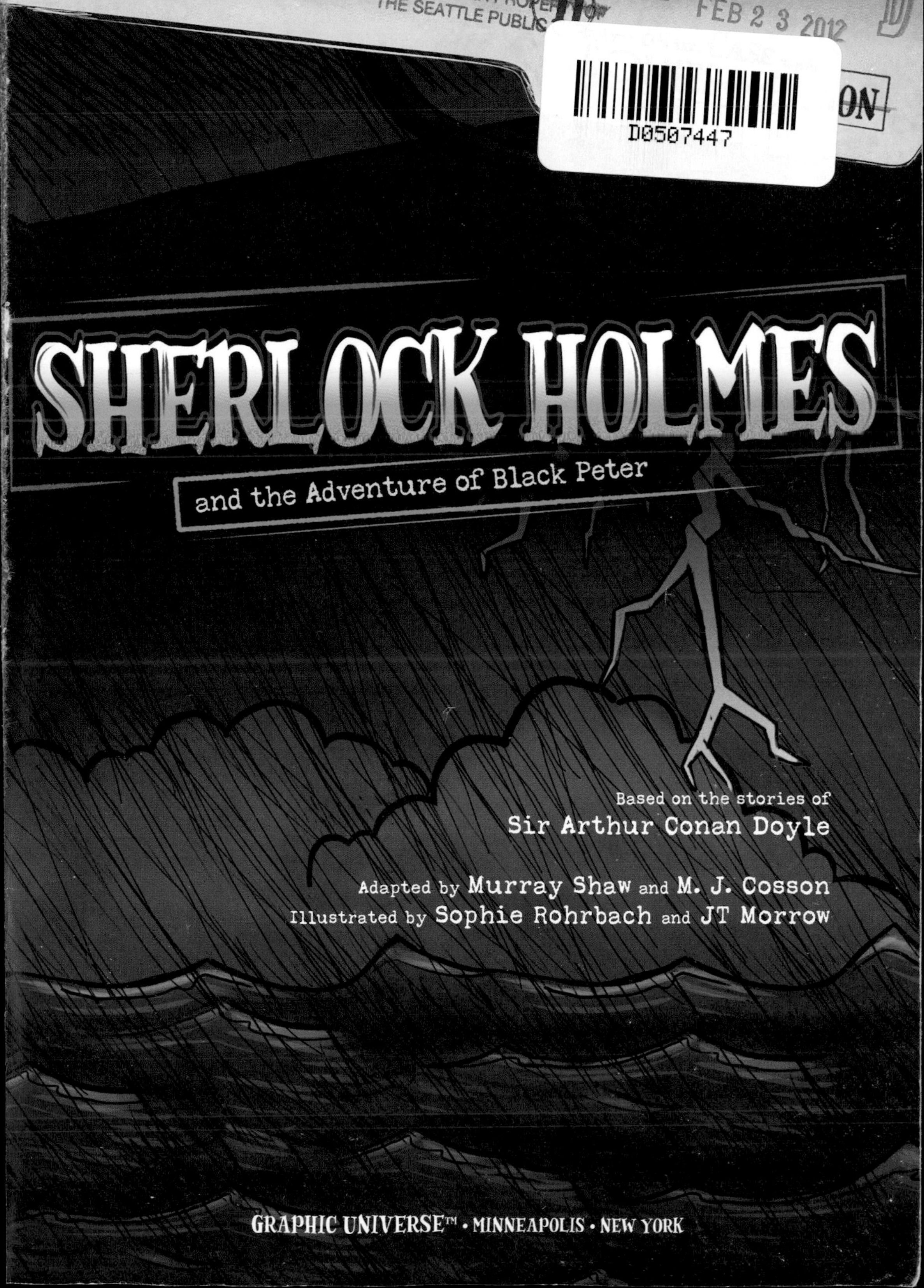

SHERLOCK HOLMES

and the Adventure of Black Peter

Based on the stories of
Sir Arthur Conan Doyle

Adapted by Murray Shaw and M. J. Cosson
Illustrated by Sophie Rohrbach and JT Morrow

GRAPHIC UNIVERSE™ • MINNEAPOLIS • NEW YORK

Grateful acknowledgment to Dame Jean Conan Doyle for permission to use the Sherlock Holmes characters created by Sir Arthur Conan Doyle

Graphic Universe™
A division of Lerner Publishing Group, Inc.
241 First Avenue North
Minneapolis, MN 55401 U.S.A.

Website address: www.lernerbooks.com

Library of Congress Cataloging-in-Publication Data

Shaw, Murray.
    Sherlock Holmes and the adventure of Black Peter / based on the stories of Sir Arthur Conan Doyle ; adapted by Murray Shaw and M. J. Cosson ; illustrated by Sophie Rohrbach and JT Morrow.
        p.   cm. — (On the case with Holmes and Watson ; #11)
    Summary: Retold in graphic novel form, Sherlock Holmes investigates the gruesome murder by harpoon of a very unpleasant former sea captain known as Black Peter. Includes a section explaining Holmes's reasoning and the clues he used to solve the mystery.
        ISBN: 978-0-7613-7092-5 (lib. bdg. : alk. paper)
        I. Graphic novels. (I. Graphic novels. 2. Doyle, Arthur Conan, Sir, 1859-1930. Adventure of Black Peter—Adaptations. 3. Mystery and detective stories.) I. Cosson, M. J. II. Rohrbach, Sophie, ill III. Morrow, JT, ill. IV. Doyle, Arthur Conan, Sir, 1859-1930. Adventure of Black Peter. V. Title.
PZ7.7.S46Shhm 2012
741.5'973—dc22   2011005115

Manufactured in the United States of America
1—BC—12/31/11

The Story of
SHERLOCK HOLMES
the Famous Detective

Sherlock Holmes and his helpful friend Dr. John Watson are fictional characters created by British writer Sir Arthur Conan Doyle. Doyle published his first novel about the pair, *A Study in Scarlet*, in 1887, and it became very successful. Doyle went on to write fifty-six short stories, as well as three more novels about Holmes's adventures—*The Sign of Four* (1890), *The Hound of the Baskervilles* (1902), and *The Valley of Fear* (1915).

Sherlock Holmes and Dr. Watson have become some of the most famous book characters of all time. Holmes spent most of his time solving mysteries, but he also had a wide array of hobbies, such as playing the violin, boxing, and sword fighting. Watson, a retired army doctor, met Holmes through a mutual friend when Holmes was looking for a roommate. Watson lived with Holmes for several years at 221B Baker Street before marrying and moving out. However, after his marriage, Watson continued to assist Holmes with his cases.

The original versions of the Sherlock Holmes stories are still printed, and many have been made into movies and television shows. Readers continue to be impressed by Holmes's detective methods of observation and scientific reason.

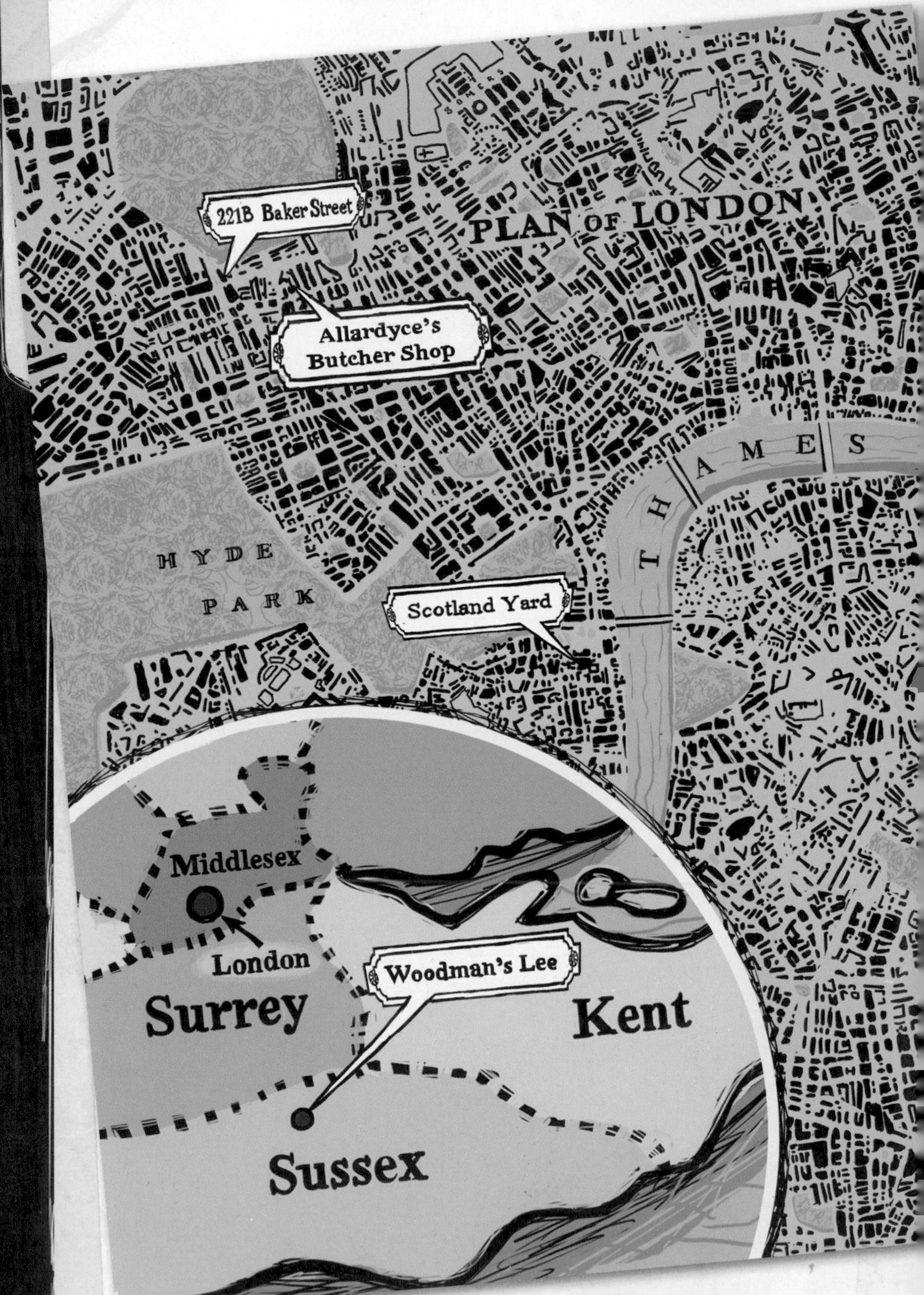
221B Baker Street
PLAN OF LONDON
Allardyce's Butcher Shop
THAMES
HYDE PARK
Scotland Yard
Middlesex
London
Woodman's Lee
Surrey
Kent
Sussex

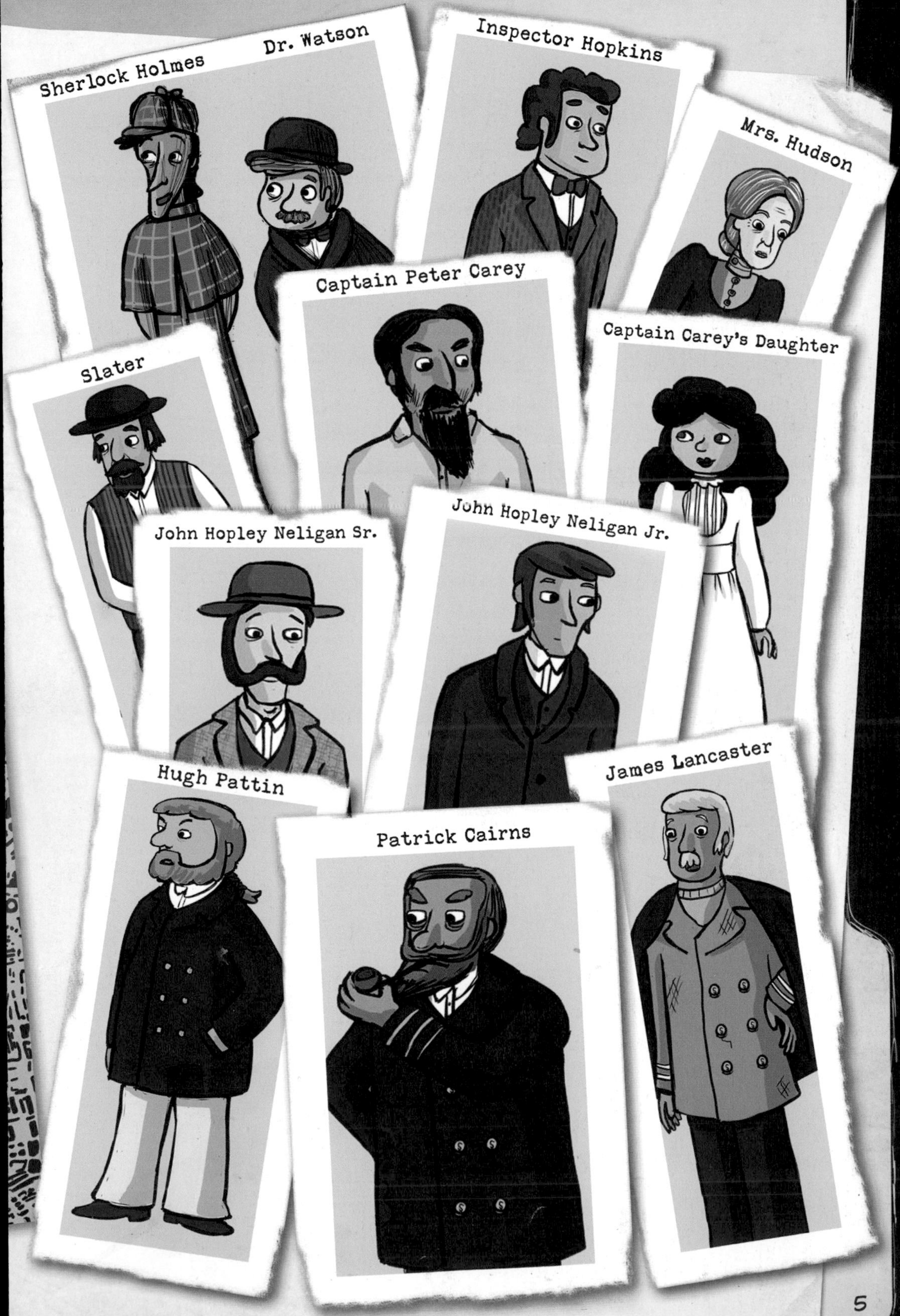
Sherlock Holmes
Dr. Watson
Inspector Hopkins
Mrs. Hudson
Captain Peter Carey
Captain Carey's Daughter
Slater
John Hopley Neligan Sr.
John Hopley Neligan Jr.
Hugh Pattin
James Lancaster
Patrick Cairns

From the Desk of John H. Watson, M.D.

My name is Dr. John H. Watson. For several years, I have been assisting my friend, Sherlock Holmes, in solving mysteries throughout the bustling city of London and beyond. Holmes is a peculiar man—always questioning and reasoning his way through various problems. But when I first met him in 1878, I was immediately intrigued by his oddities.

Holmes has always been more daring than I, and his logical deduction never ceases to amaze me. I have begun writing down all of the adventures I have with Holmes. This is one of those stories.

Sincerely,

Dr. Watson

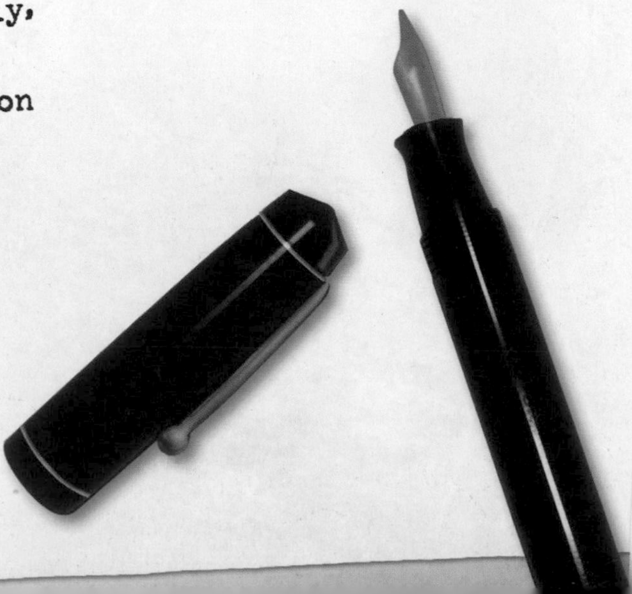

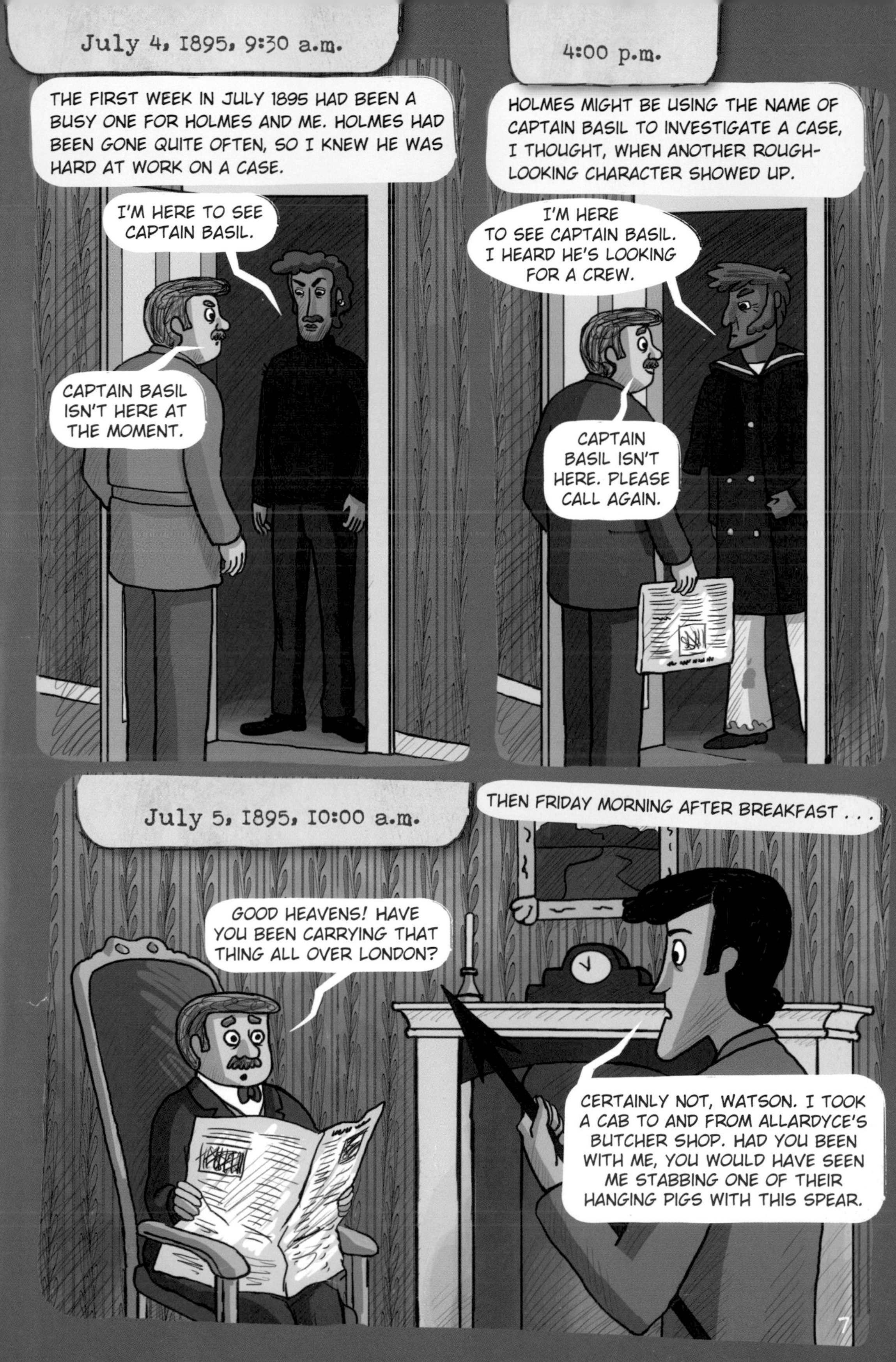
July 4, 1895, 9:30 a.m.
THE FIRST WEEK IN JULY 1895 HAD BEEN A BUSY ONE FOR HOLMES AND ME. HOLMES HAD BEEN GONE QUITE OFTEN, SO I KNEW HE WAS HARD AT WORK ON A CASE.
I'M HERE TO SEE CAPTAIN BASIL.
CAPTAIN BASIL ISN'T HERE AT THE MOMENT.
4:00 p.m.
HOLMES MIGHT BE USING THE NAME OF CAPTAIN BASIL TO INVESTIGATE A CASE, I THOUGHT, WHEN ANOTHER ROUGH-LOOKING CHARACTER SHOWED UP.
I'M HERE TO SEE CAPTAIN BASIL. I HEARD HE'S LOOKING FOR A CREW.
CAPTAIN BASIL ISN'T HERE. PLEASE CALL AGAIN.
July 5, 1895, 10:00 a.m.
THEN FRIDAY MORNING AFTER BREAKFAST . . .
GOOD HEAVENS! HAVE YOU BEEN CARRYING THAT THING ALL OVER LONDON?
CERTAINLY NOT, WATSON. I TOOK A CAB TO AND FROM ALLARDYCE'S BUTCHER SHOP. HAD YOU BEEN WITH ME, YOU WOULD HAVE SEEN ME STABBING ONE OF THEIR HANGING PIGS WITH THIS SPEAR.

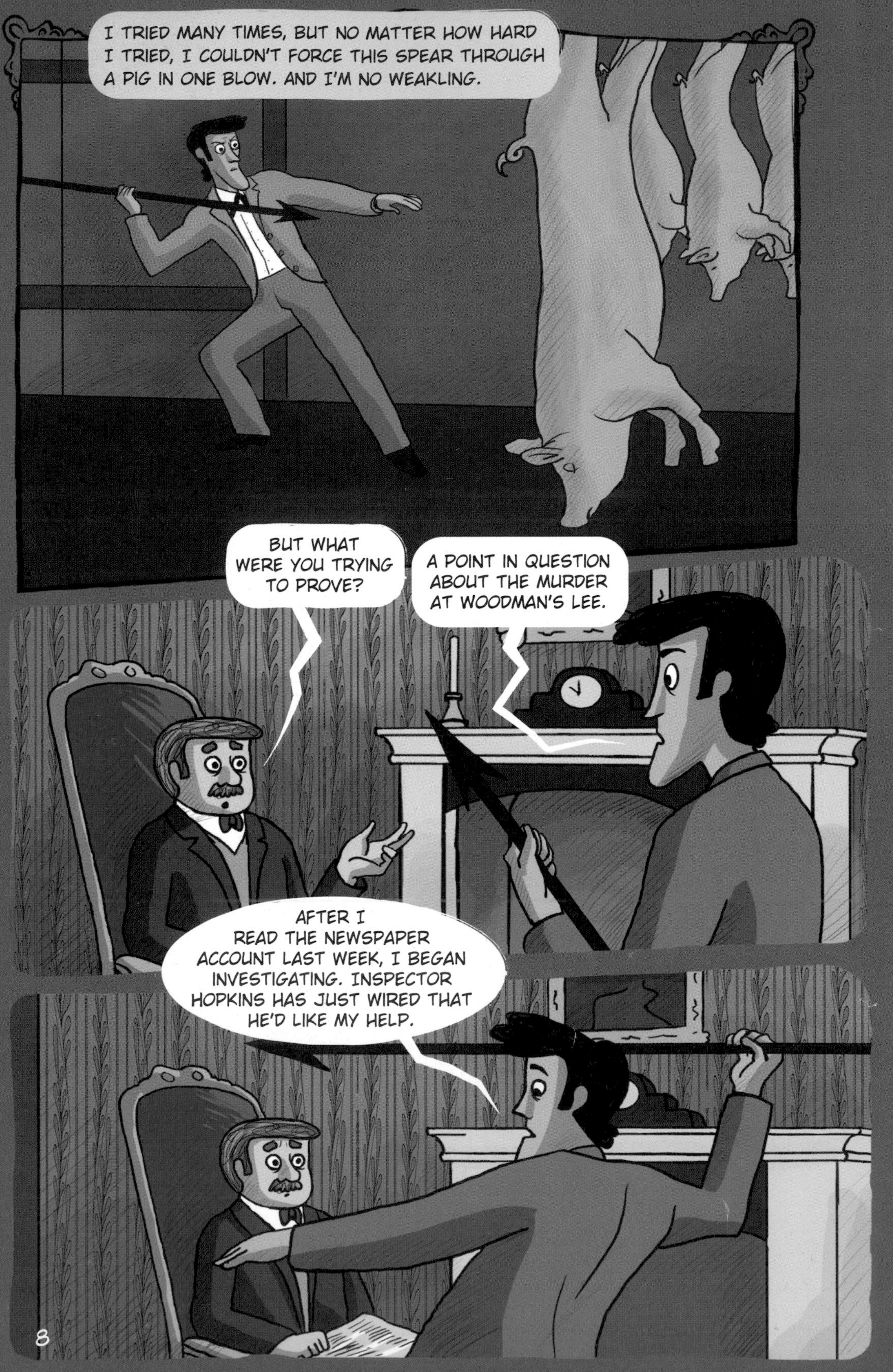
I TRIED MANY TIMES, BUT NO MATTER HOW HARD I TRIED, I COULDN'T FORCE THIS SPEAR THROUGH A PIG IN ONE BLOW. AND I'M NO WEAKLING.
BUT WHAT WERE YOU TRYING TO PROVE?
A POINT IN QUESTION ABOUT THE MURDER AT WOODMAN'S LEE.
AFTER I READ THE NEWSPAPER ACCOUNT LAST WEEK, I BEGAN INVESTIGATING. INSPECTOR HOPKINS HAS JUST WIRED THAT HE'D LIKE MY HELP.

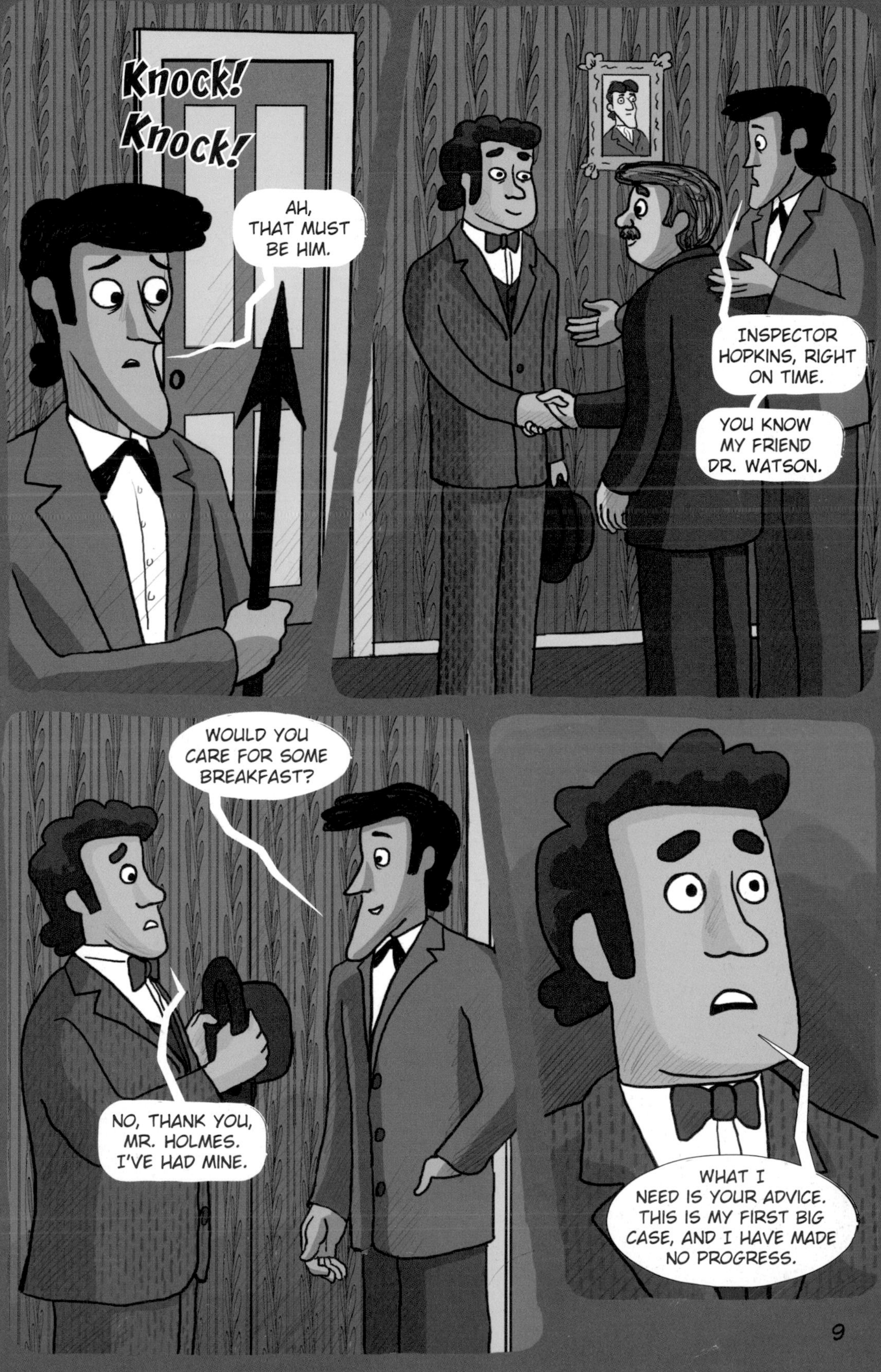
Knock! Knock!
AH, THAT MUST BE HIM.
INSPECTOR HOPKINS, RIGHT ON TIME.
YOU KNOW MY FRIEND DR. WATSON.
WOULD YOU CARE FOR SOME BREAKFAST?
NO, THANK YOU, MR. HOLMES. I'VE HAD MINE.
WHAT I NEED IS YOUR ADVICE. THIS IS MY FIRST BIG CASE, AND I HAVE MADE NO PROGRESS.

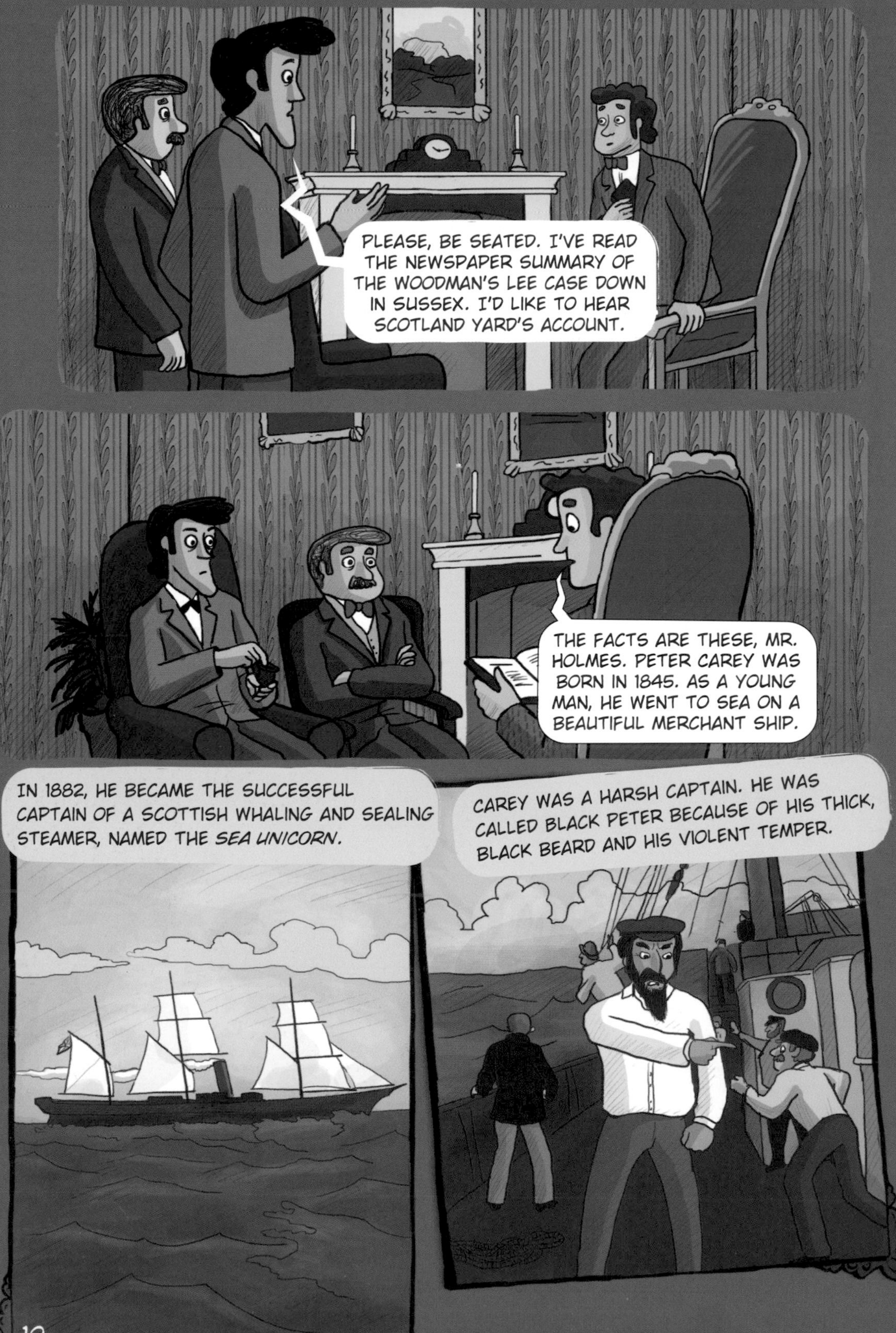
PLEASE, BE SEATED. I'VE READ THE NEWSPAPER SUMMARY OF THE WOODMAN'S LEE CASE DOWN IN SUSSEX. I'D LIKE TO HEAR SCOTLAND YARD'S ACCOUNT.
THE FACTS ARE THESE, MR. HOLMES. PETER CAREY WAS BORN IN 1845. AS A YOUNG MAN, HE WENT TO SEA ON A BEAUTIFUL MERCHANT SHIP.
IN 1882, HE BECAME THE SUCCESSFUL CAPTAIN OF A SCOTTISH WHALING AND SEALING STEAMER, NAMED THE *SEA UNICORN*.
CAREY WAS A HARSH CAPTAIN. HE WAS CALLED BLACK PETER BECAUSE OF HIS THICK, BLACK BEARD AND HIS VIOLENT TEMPER.

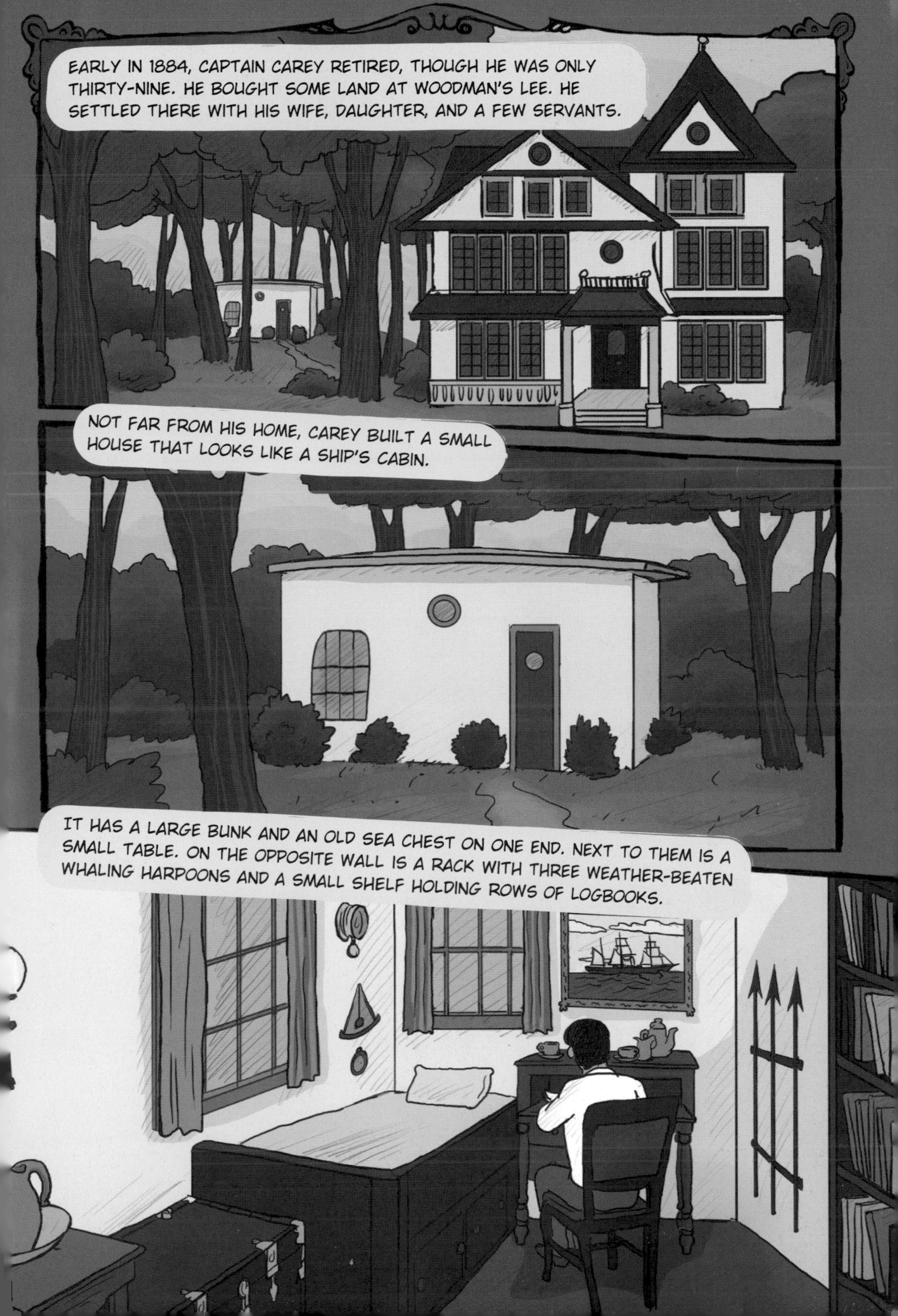
EARLY IN 1884, CAPTAIN CAREY RETIRED, THOUGH HE WAS ONLY THIRTY-NINE. HE BOUGHT SOME LAND AT WOODMAN'S LEE. HE SETTLED THERE WITH HIS WIFE, DAUGHTER, AND A FEW SERVANTS.
NOT FAR FROM HIS HOME, CAREY BUILT A SMALL HOUSE THAT LOOKS LIKE A SHIP'S CABIN.
IT HAS A LARGE BUNK AND AN OLD SEA CHEST ON ONE END. NEXT TO THEM IS A SMALL TABLE. ON THE OPPOSITE WALL IS A RACK WITH THREE WEATHER-BEATEN WHALING HARPOONS AND A SMALL SHELF HOLDING ROWS OF LOGBOOKS.

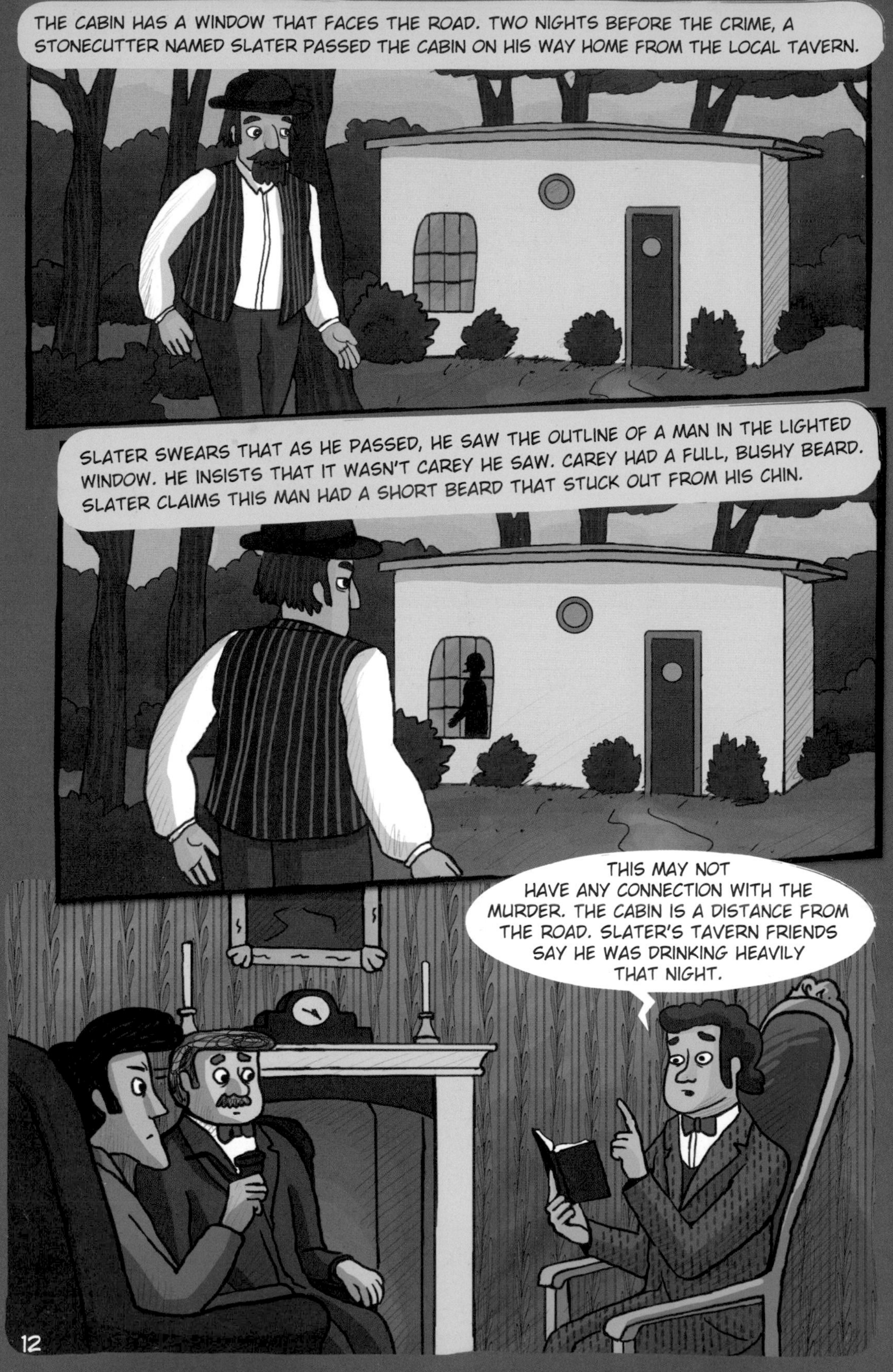
THE CABIN HAS A WINDOW THAT FACES THE ROAD. TWO NIGHTS BEFORE THE CRIME, A STONECUTTER NAMED SLATER PASSED THE CABIN ON HIS WAY HOME FROM THE LOCAL TAVERN.
SLATER SWEARS THAT AS HE PASSED, HE SAW THE OUTLINE OF A MAN IN THE LIGHTED WINDOW. HE INSISTS THAT IT WASN'T CAREY HE SAW. CAREY HAD A FULL, BUSHY BEARD. SLATER CLAIMS THIS MAN HAD A SHORT BEARD THAT STUCK OUT FROM HIS CHIN.
THIS MAY NOT HAVE ANY CONNECTION WITH THE MURDER. THE CABIN IS A DISTANCE FROM THE ROAD. SLATER'S TAVERN FRIENDS SAY HE WAS DRINKING HEAVILY THAT NIGHT.

LATE ON THE NIGHT OF HIS TERRIBLE DEATH, CAREY STAGGERED TO HIS CABIN. HE HAD BEEN ANGRY ALL DAY.

SOMETIME IN THE MIDDLE OF THAT NIGHT, HIS DAUGHTER WAS AWAKENED BY A PIERCING CRY. BUT SHE WAS USED TO HER FATHER'S RAGES. SHE WENT BACK TO SLEEP AND THOUGHT NO MORE ABOUT IT.

AAAAAAGGGGHHHHHH!

THE NEXT MORNING, ONE OF THE MAIDS NOTICED THE CABIN DOOR WAS OPEN. SHE APPROACHED AND PEERED IN. THEN SHE WENT OFF SCREAMING, AND I WAS SENT FOR.

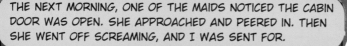

AAAHHHH!

GENTLEMEN, I HAVE STEADY NERVES, BUT NO SOLDIER'S TRAINING COULD HAVE PREPARED ME FOR THE SIGHT IN THAT CABIN.

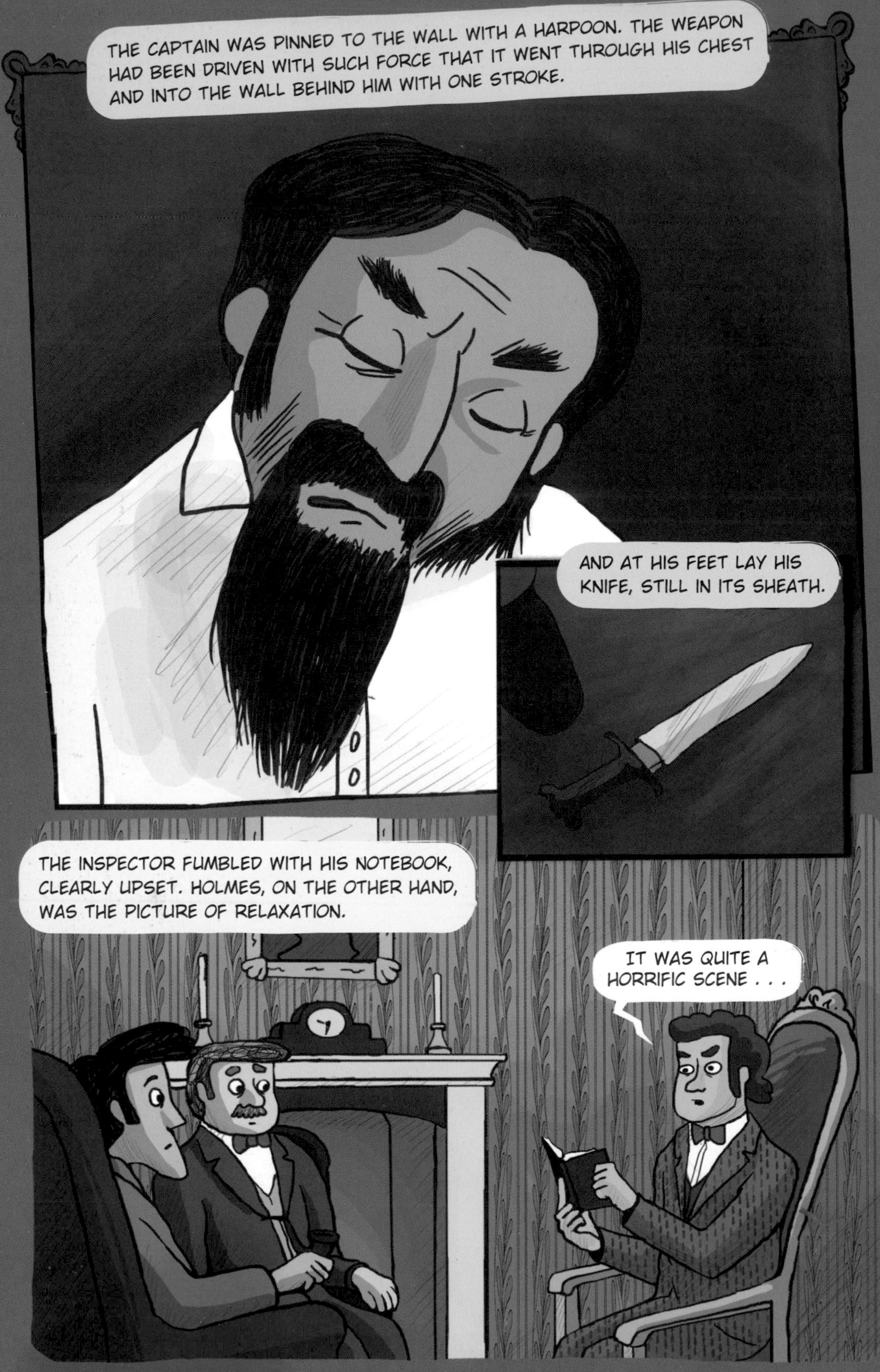
THE CAPTAIN WAS PINNED TO THE WALL WITH A HARPOON. THE WEAPON HAD BEEN DRIVEN WITH SUCH FORCE THAT IT WENT THROUGH HIS CHEST AND INTO THE WALL BEHIND HIM WITH ONE STROKE.
AND AT HIS FEET LAY HIS KNIFE, STILL IN ITS SHEATH.
THE INSPECTOR FUMBLED WITH HIS NOTEBOOK, CLEARLY UPSET. HOLMES, ON THE OTHER HAND, WAS THE PICTURE OF RELAXATION.
IT WAS QUITE A HORRIFIC SCENE . . .

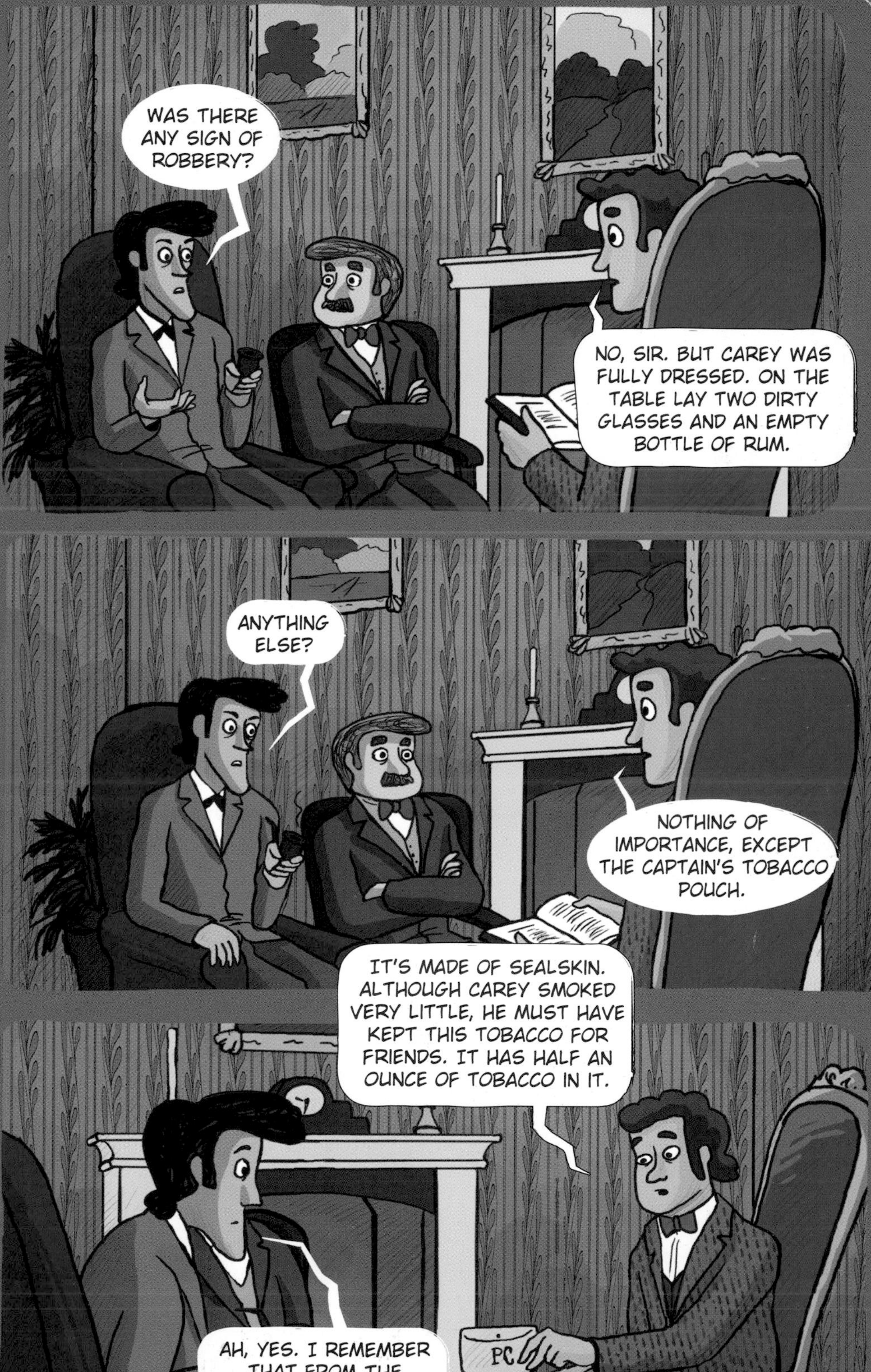
WAS THERE ANY SIGN OF ROBBERY?
NO, SIR. BUT CAREY WAS FULLY DRESSED. ON THE TABLE LAY TWO DIRTY GLASSES AND AN EMPTY BOTTLE OF RUM.
ANYTHING ELSE?
NOTHING OF IMPORTANCE, EXCEPT THE CAPTAIN'S TOBACCO POUCH.
IT'S MADE OF SEALSKIN. ALTHOUGH CAREY SMOKED VERY LITTLE, HE MUST HAVE KEPT THIS TOBACCO FOR FRIENDS. IT HAS HALF AN OUNCE OF TOBACCO IN IT.
PC
AH, YES. I REMEMBER THAT FROM THE NEWSPAPER ACCOUNT.

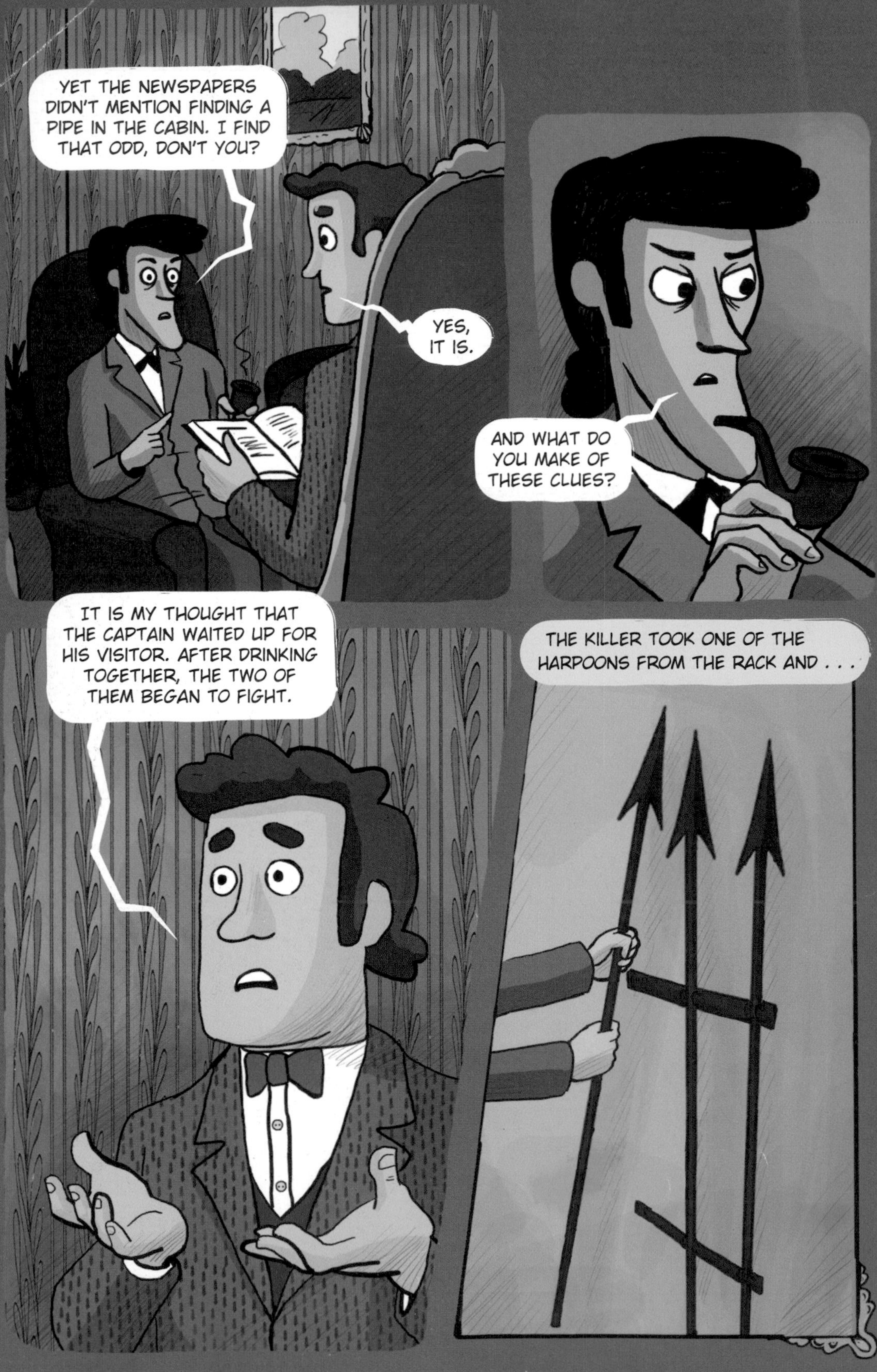
YET THE NEWSPAPERS DIDN'T MENTION FINDING A PIPE IN THE CABIN. I FIND THAT ODD, DON'T YOU?
YES, IT IS.
AND WHAT DO YOU MAKE OF THESE CLUES?
IT IS MY THOUGHT THAT THE CAPTAIN WAITED UP FOR HIS VISITOR. AFTER DRINKING TOGETHER, THE TWO OF THEM BEGAN TO FIGHT.
THE KILLER TOOK ONE OF THE HARPOONS FROM THE RACK AND . . .

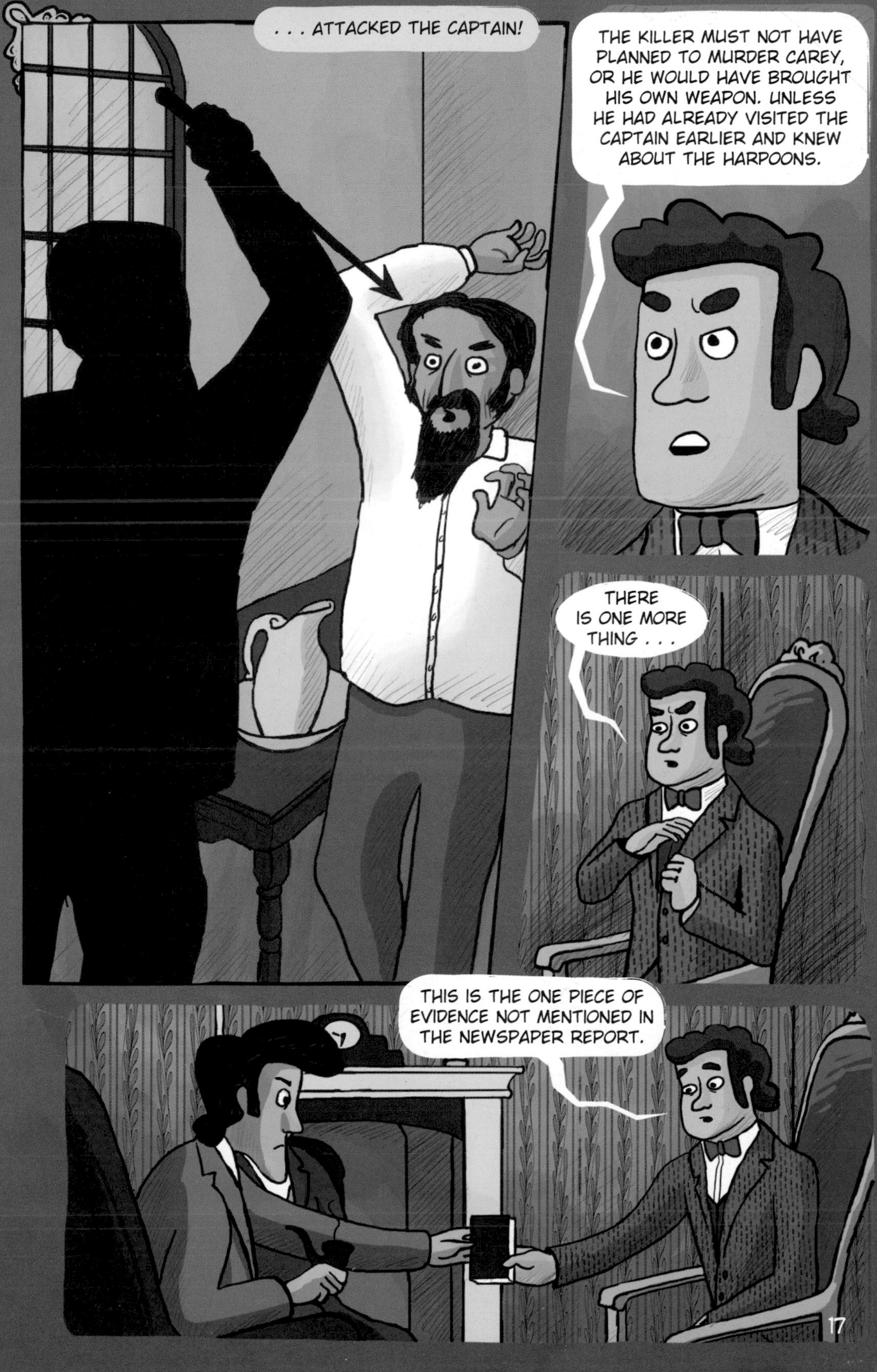

. . . ATTACKED THE CAPTAIN!
THE KILLER MUST NOT HAVE PLANNED TO MURDER CAREY, OR HE WOULD HAVE BROUGHT HIS OWN WEAPON. UNLESS HE HAD ALREADY VISITED THE CAPTAIN EARLIER AND KNEW ABOUT THE HARPOONS.
THERE IS ONE MORE THING . . .
THIS IS THE ONE PIECE OF EVIDENCE NOT MENTIONED IN THE NEWSPAPER REPORT.

Holmes examined the notebook. Handwritten on the first page were the initials J.H.N. and the year 1883. On the pages that followed were headings, such as C.P.R., Argentina, and Australia. Beneath each heading was a list of numbers or company names.

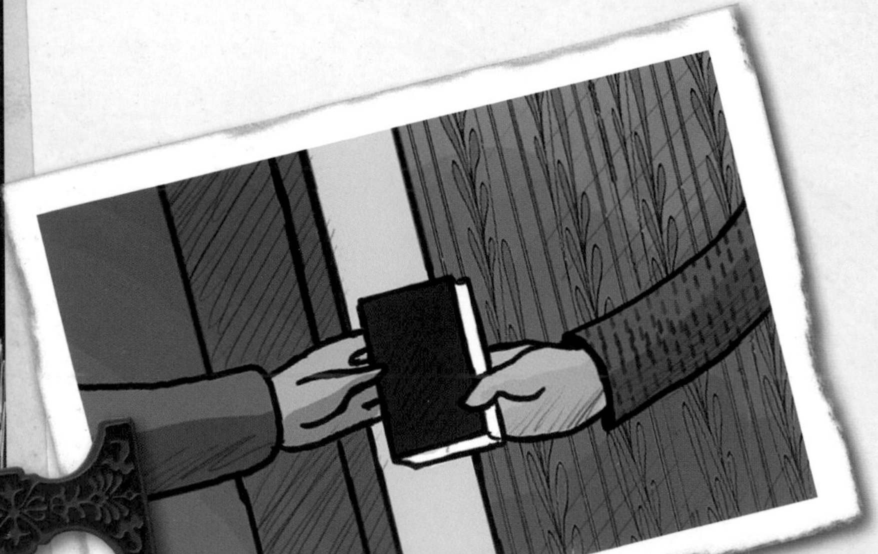

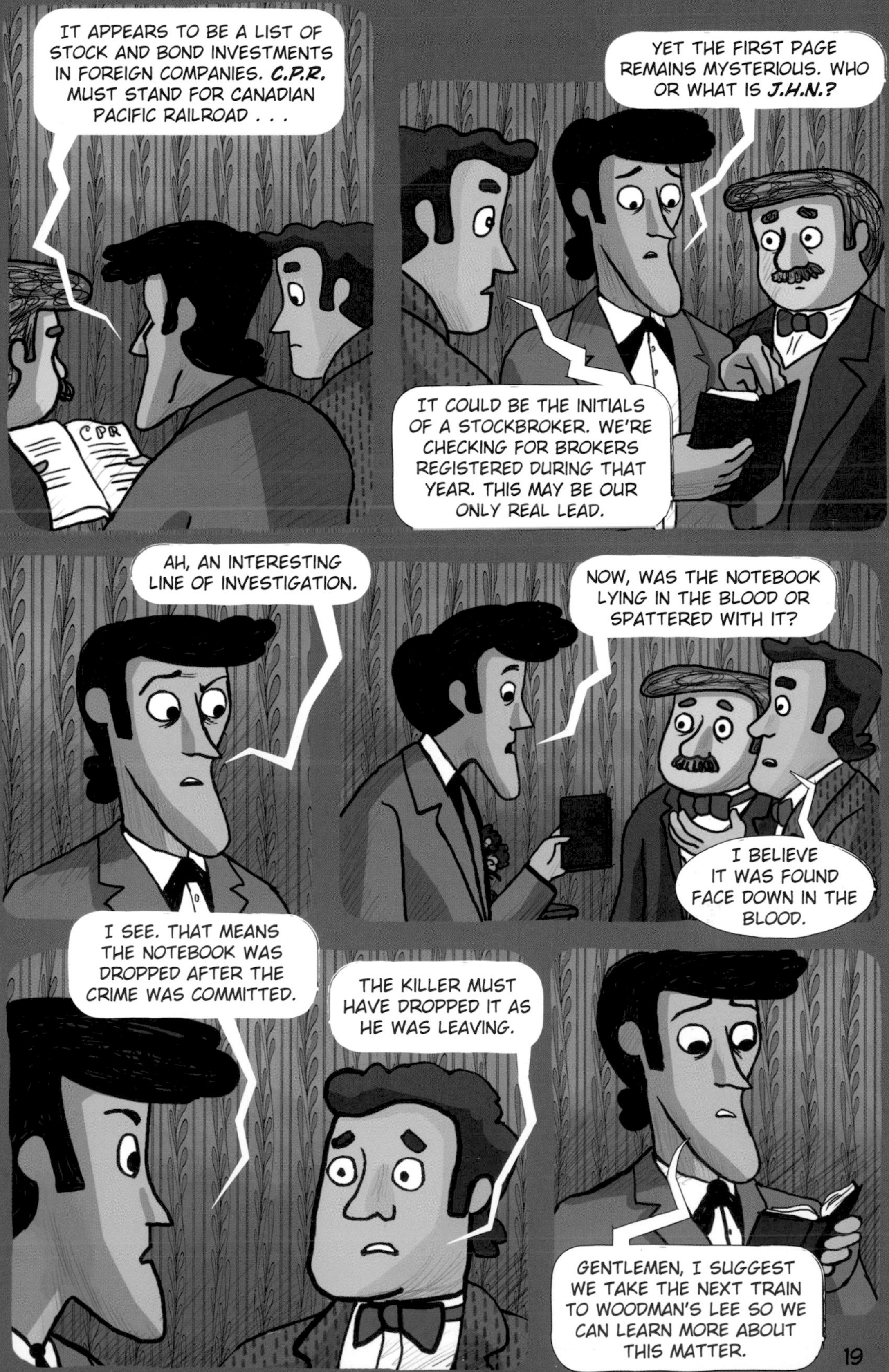
IT APPEARS TO BE A LIST OF STOCK AND BOND INVESTMENTS IN FOREIGN COMPANIES. ***C.P.R.*** MUST STAND FOR CANADIAN PACIFIC RAILROAD . . .
CPR
YET THE FIRST PAGE REMAINS MYSTERIOUS. WHO OR WHAT IS ***J.H.N.?***
IT COULD BE THE INITIALS OF A STOCKBROKER. WE'RE CHECKING FOR BROKERS REGISTERED DURING THAT YEAR. THIS MAY BE OUR ONLY REAL LEAD.
AH, AN INTERESTING LINE OF INVESTIGATION.
NOW, WAS THE NOTEBOOK LYING IN THE BLOOD OR SPATTERED WITH IT?
I BELIEVE IT WAS FOUND FACE DOWN IN THE BLOOD.
I SEE. THAT MEANS THE NOTEBOOK WAS DROPPED AFTER THE CRIME WAS COMMITTED.
THE KILLER MUST HAVE DROPPED IT AS HE WAS LEAVING.
GENTLEMEN, I SUGGEST WE TAKE THE NEXT TRAIN TO WOODMAN'S LEE SO WE CAN LEARN MORE ABOUT THIS MATTER.

That afternoon, after arriving at the train station in the village of Woodman's Lee, we took a carriage to Carey's house. His wife and daughter greeted us. They gave us permission to examine the cabin but refused to come with us. Taking the well-worn path, we headed through the woods to the one-room cabin.

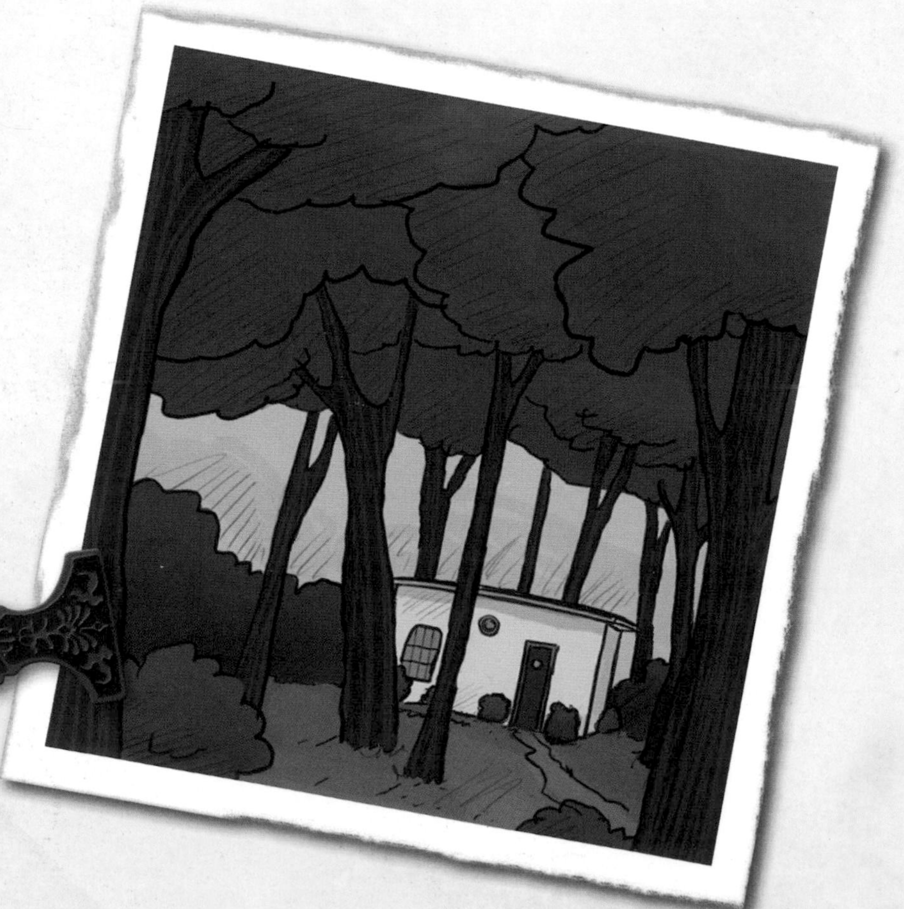

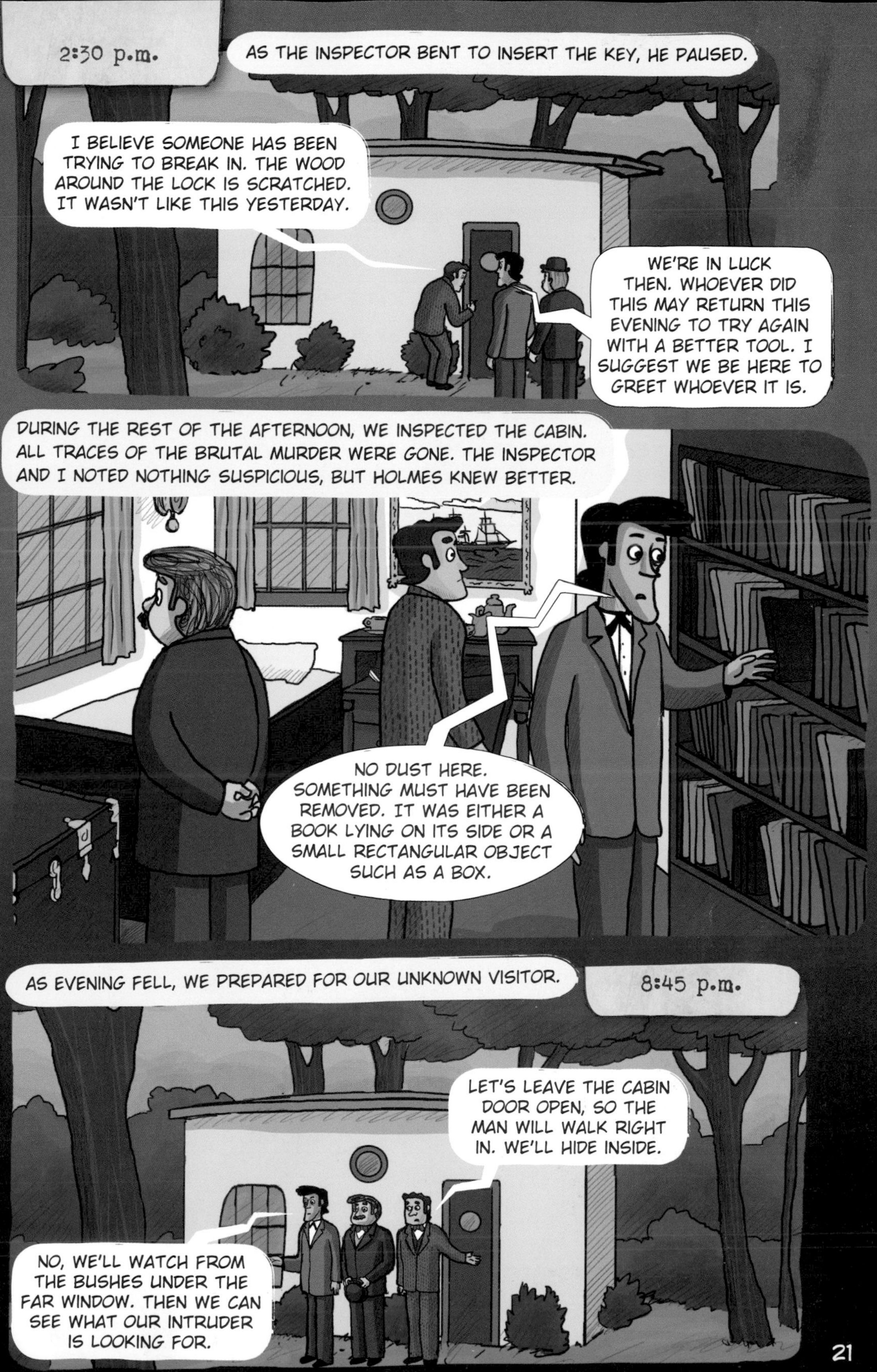
2:30 p.m.
AS THE INSPECTOR BENT TO INSERT THE KEY, HE PAUSED.
I BELIEVE SOMEONE HAS BEEN TRYING TO BREAK IN. THE WOOD AROUND THE LOCK IS SCRATCHED. IT WASN'T LIKE THIS YESTERDAY.
WE'RE IN LUCK THEN. WHOEVER DID THIS MAY RETURN THIS EVENING TO TRY AGAIN WITH A BETTER TOOL. I SUGGEST WE BE HERE TO GREET WHOEVER IT IS.
DURING THE REST OF THE AFTERNOON, WE INSPECTED THE CABIN. ALL TRACES OF THE BRUTAL MURDER WERE GONE. THE INSPECTOR AND I NOTED NOTHING SUSPICIOUS, BUT HOLMES KNEW BETTER.
NO DUST HERE. SOMETHING MUST HAVE BEEN REMOVED. IT WAS EITHER A BOOK LYING ON ITS SIDE OR A SMALL RECTANGULAR OBJECT SUCH AS A BOX.
AS EVENING FELL, WE PREPARED FOR OUR UNKNOWN VISITOR.
8:45 p.m.
LET'S LEAVE THE CABIN DOOR OPEN, SO THE MAN WILL WALK RIGHT IN. WE'LL HIDE INSIDE.
NO, WE'LL WATCH FROM THE BUSHES UNDER THE FAR WINDOW. THEN WE CAN SEE WHAT OUR INTRUDER IS LOOKING FOR.

It was a gloomy task to crouch among the bushes through the sunset and oncoming night. Yet there was a kind of strange thrill to it all—such as a hunter feels. What murderous beast would we meet in the darkness? What raging fight would it take to capture the creature?

A fine drizzle began to fall, and over the sound of the rain on the leaves, we could hear the church bells chime—first midnight, then one o'clock, and then two. Each time a villager passed on the road, we would stiffen and wait for approaching steps.

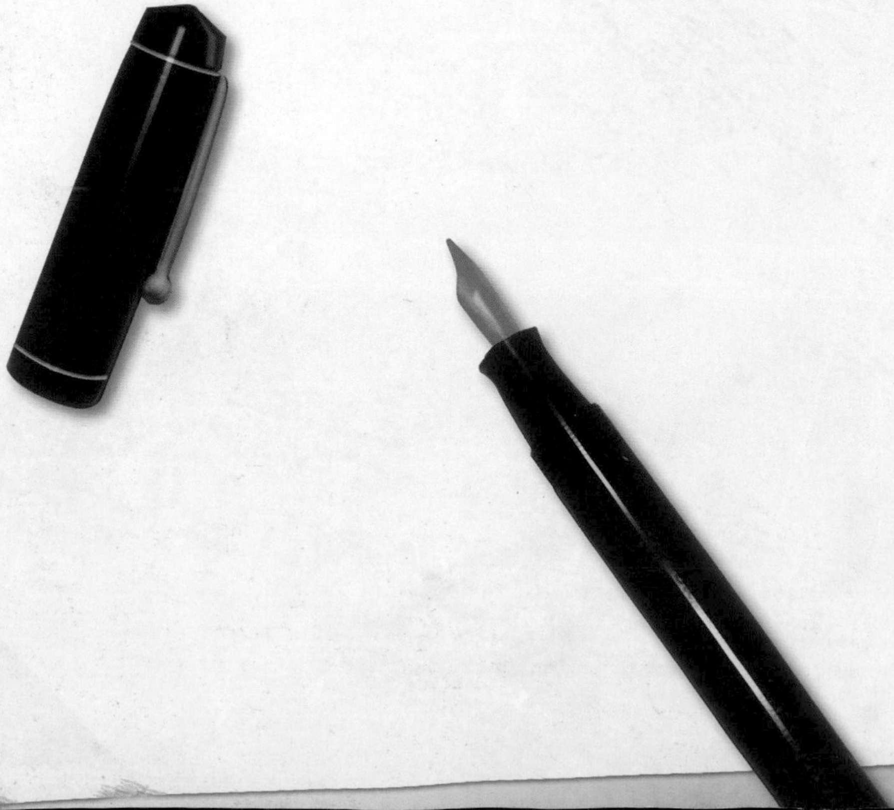

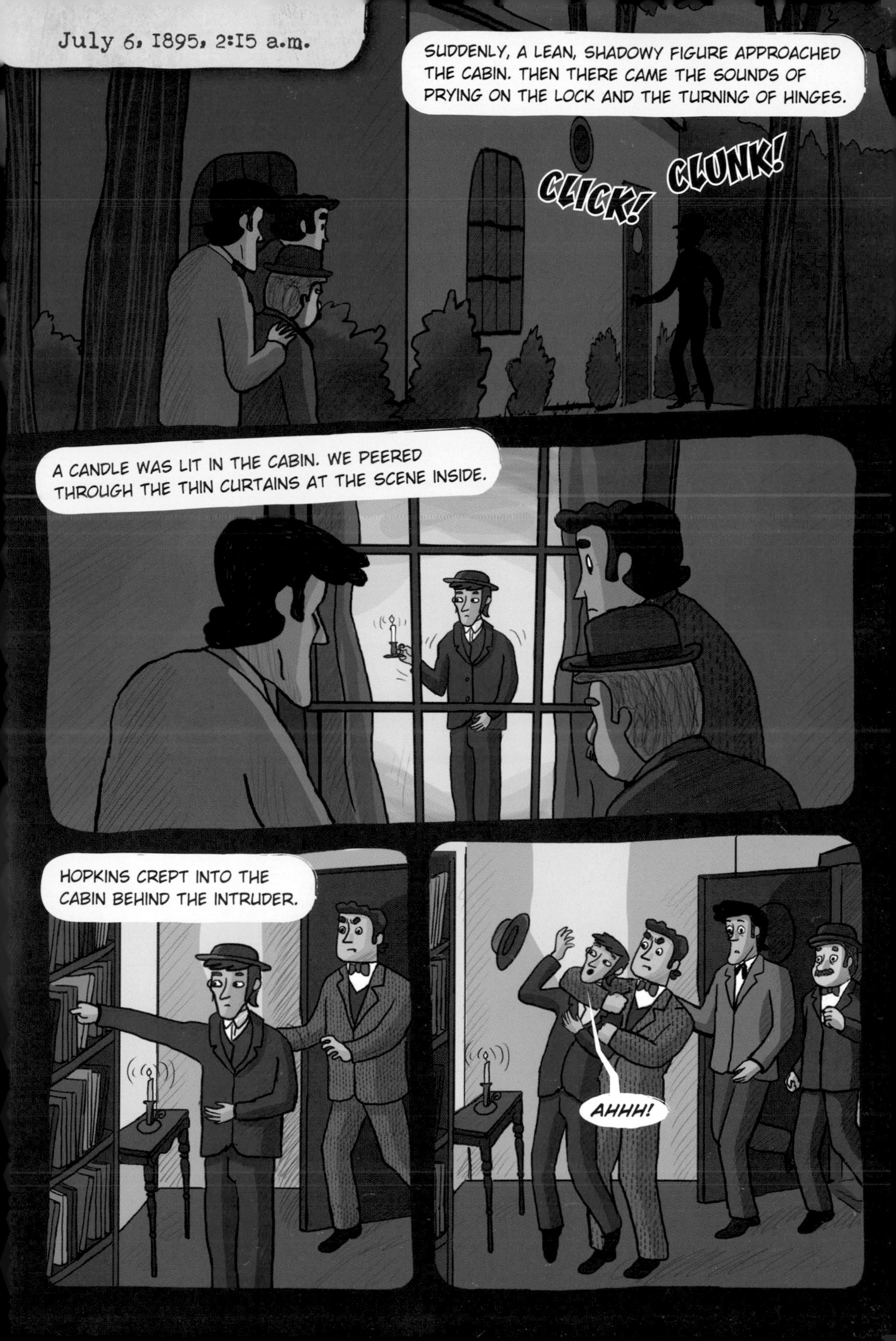

July 6, 1895, 2:15 a.m.
SUDDENLY, A LEAN, SHADOWY FIGURE APPROACHED THE CABIN. THEN THERE CAME THE SOUNDS OF PRYING ON THE LOCK AND THE TURNING OF HINGES.
CLICK!
CLUNK!
A CANDLE WAS LIT IN THE CABIN. WE PEERED THROUGH THE THIN CURTAINS AT THE SCENE INSIDE.
HOPKINS CREPT INTO THE CABIN BEHIND THE INTRUDER.
AHHH!

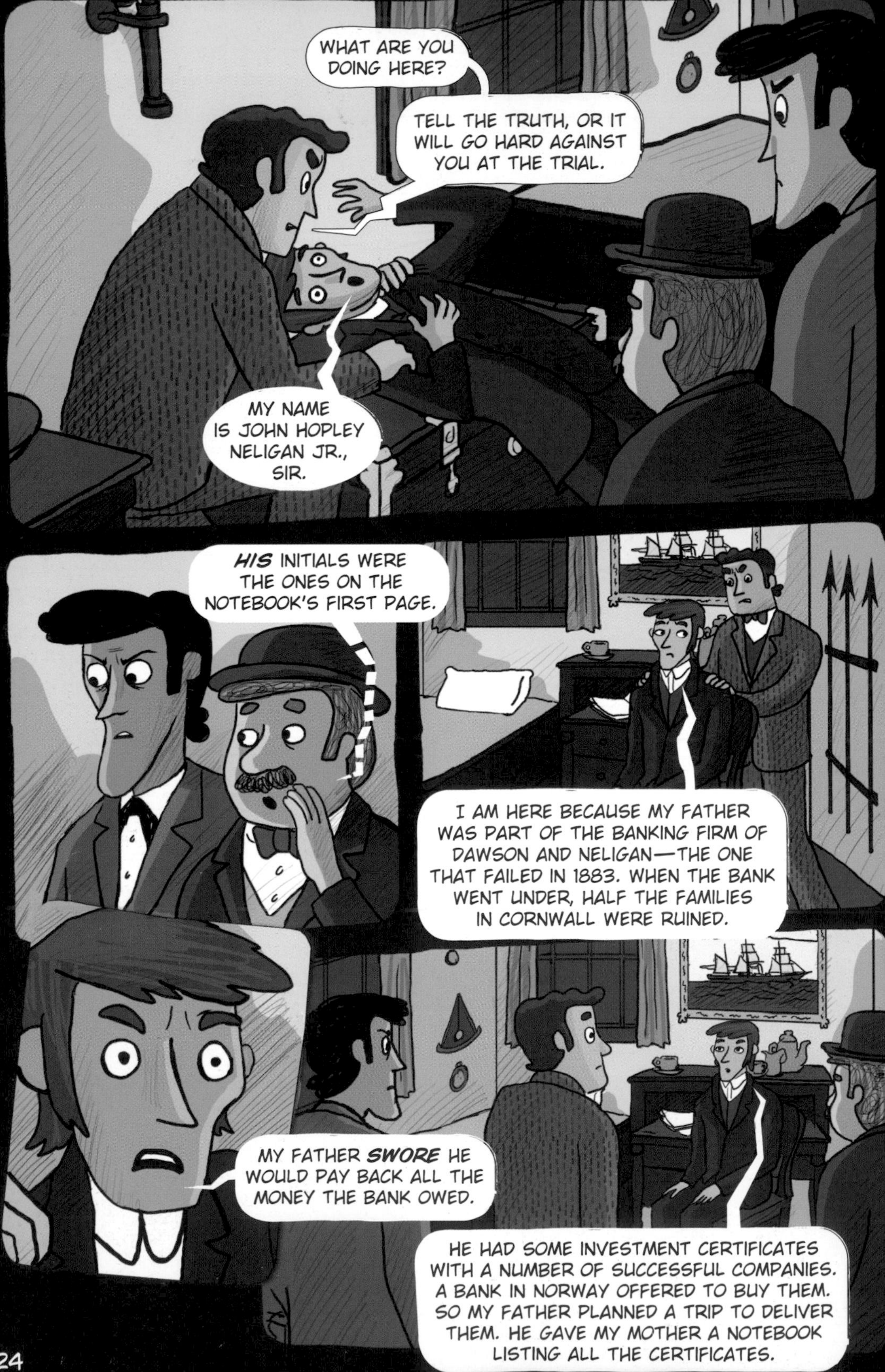
WHAT ARE YOU DOING HERE?
TELL THE TRUTH, OR IT WILL GO HARD AGAINST YOU AT THE TRIAL.
MY NAME IS JOHN HOPLEY NELIGAN JR., SIR.
HIS INITIALS WERE THE ONES ON THE NOTEBOOK'S FIRST PAGE.
I AM HERE BECAUSE MY FATHER WAS PART OF THE BANKING FIRM OF DAWSON AND NELIGAN—THE ONE THAT FAILED IN 1883. WHEN THE BANK WENT UNDER, HALF THE FAMILIES IN CORNWALL WERE RUINED.
MY FATHER SWORE HE WOULD PAY BACK ALL THE MONEY THE BANK OWED.
HE HAD SOME INVESTMENT CERTIFICATES WITH A NUMBER OF SUCCESSFUL COMPANIES. A BANK IN NORWAY OFFERED TO BUY THEM. SO MY FATHER PLANNED A TRIP TO DELIVER THEM. HE GAVE MY MOTHER A NOTEBOOK LISTING ALL THE CERTIFICATES.

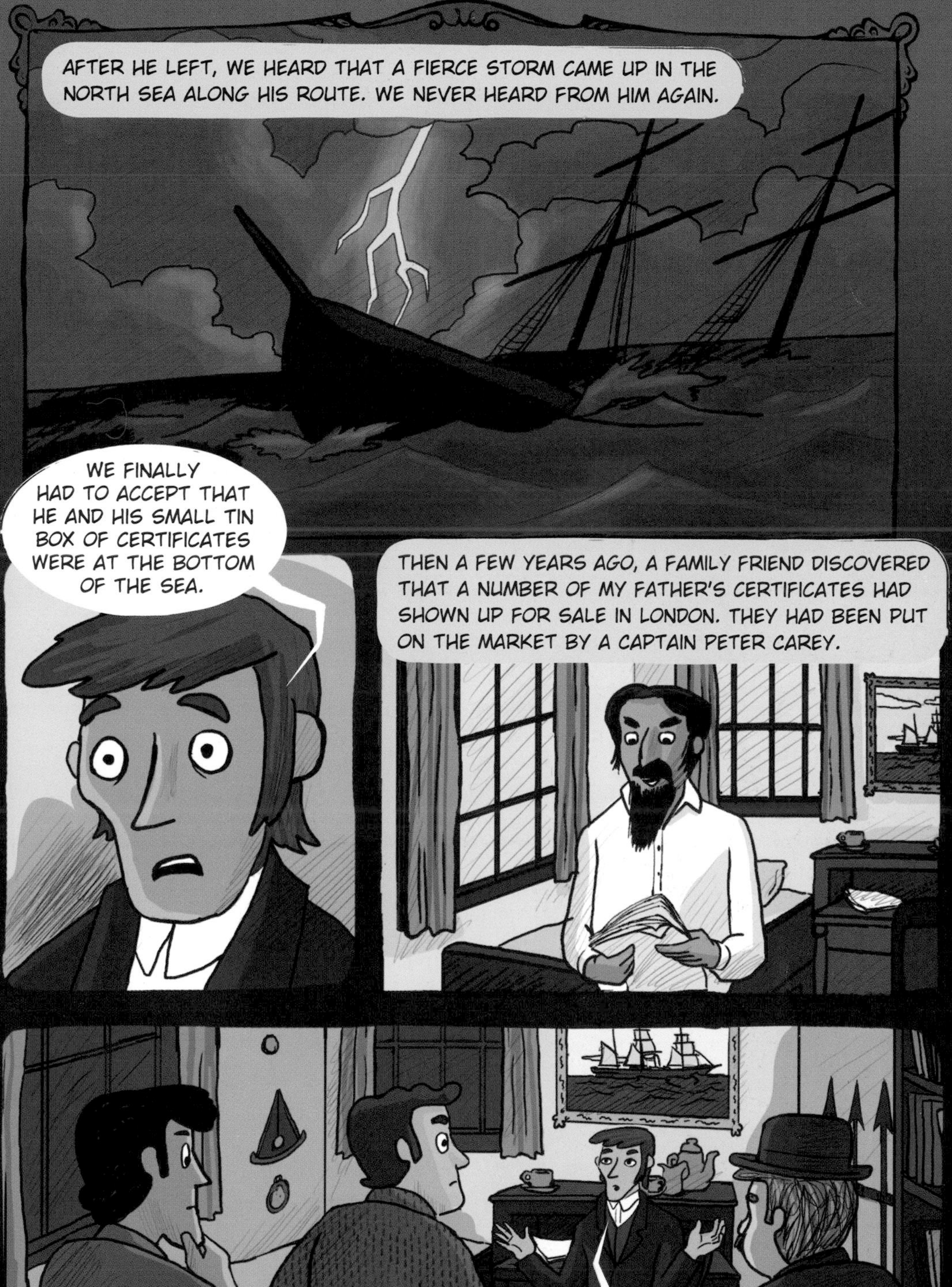
AFTER HE LEFT, WE HEARD THAT A FIERCE STORM CAME UP IN THE NORTH SEA ALONG HIS ROUTE. WE NEVER HEARD FROM HIM AGAIN.
WE FINALLY HAD TO ACCEPT THAT HE AND HIS SMALL TIN BOX OF CERTIFICATES WERE AT THE BOTTOM OF THE SEA.
THEN A FEW YEARS AGO, A FAMILY FRIEND DISCOVERED THAT A NUMBER OF MY FATHER'S CERTIFICATES HAD SHOWN UP FOR SALE IN LONDON. THEY HAD BEEN PUT ON THE MARKET BY A CAPTAIN PETER CAREY.
I FIGURED THE CAPTAIN MUST KNOW SOMETHING ABOUT MY FATHER IF HE HAD THE CERTIFICATES. SO I TRACKED HIM HERE.

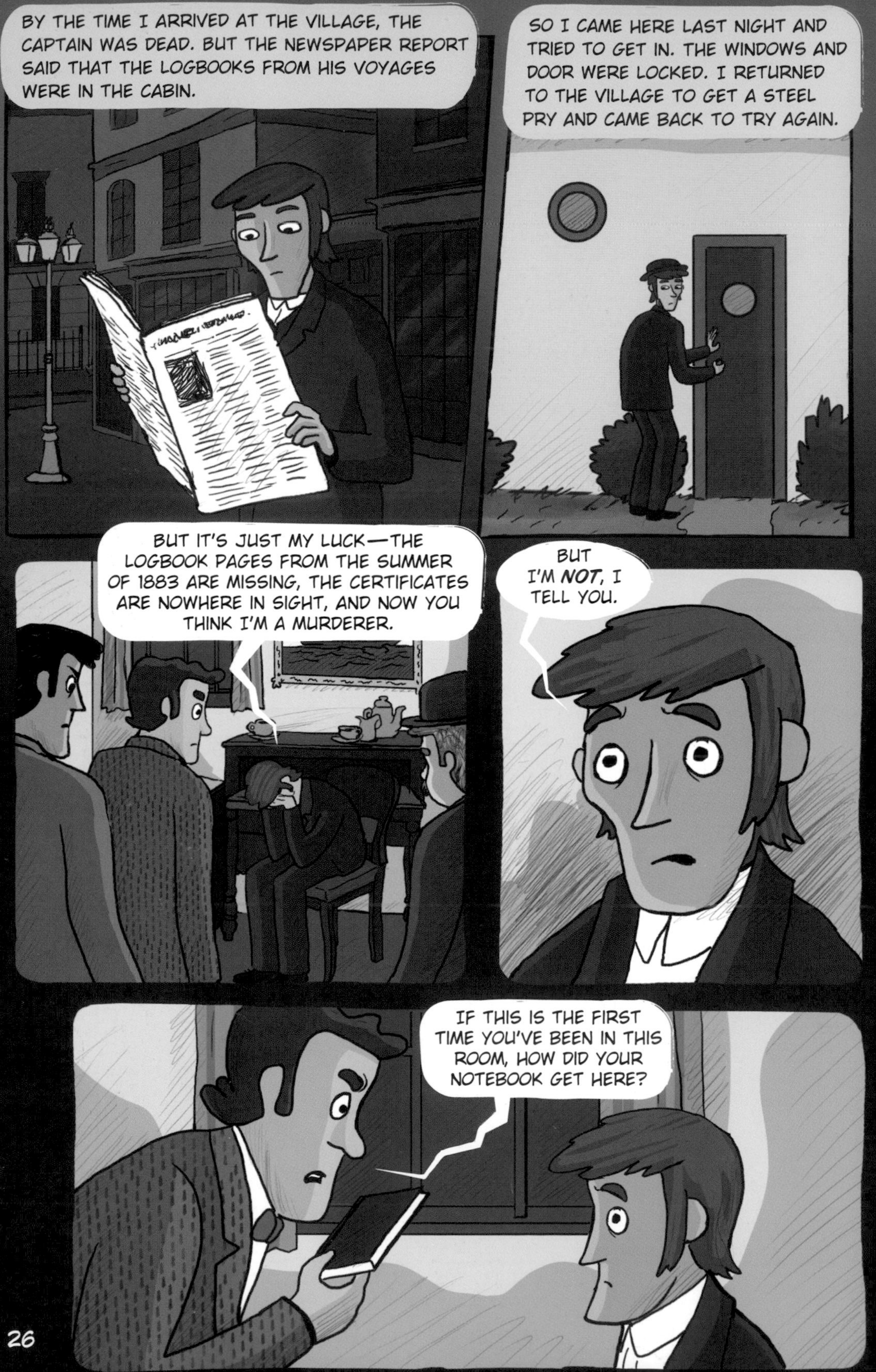
BY THE TIME I ARRIVED AT THE VILLAGE, THE CAPTAIN WAS DEAD. BUT THE NEWSPAPER REPORT SAID THAT THE LOGBOOKS FROM HIS VOYAGES WERE IN THE CABIN.
SO I CAME HERE LAST NIGHT AND TRIED TO GET IN. THE WINDOWS AND DOOR WERE LOCKED. I RETURNED TO THE VILLAGE TO GET A STEEL PRY AND CAME BACK TO TRY AGAIN.
BUT IT'S JUST MY LUCK—THE LOGBOOK PAGES FROM THE SUMMER OF 1883 ARE MISSING, THE CERTIFICATES ARE NOWHERE IN SIGHT, AND NOW YOU THINK I'M A MURDERER.
BUT I'M ***NOT***, I TELL YOU.
IF THIS IS THE FIRST TIME YOU'VE BEEN IN THIS ROOM, HOW DID YOUR NOTEBOOK GET HERE?

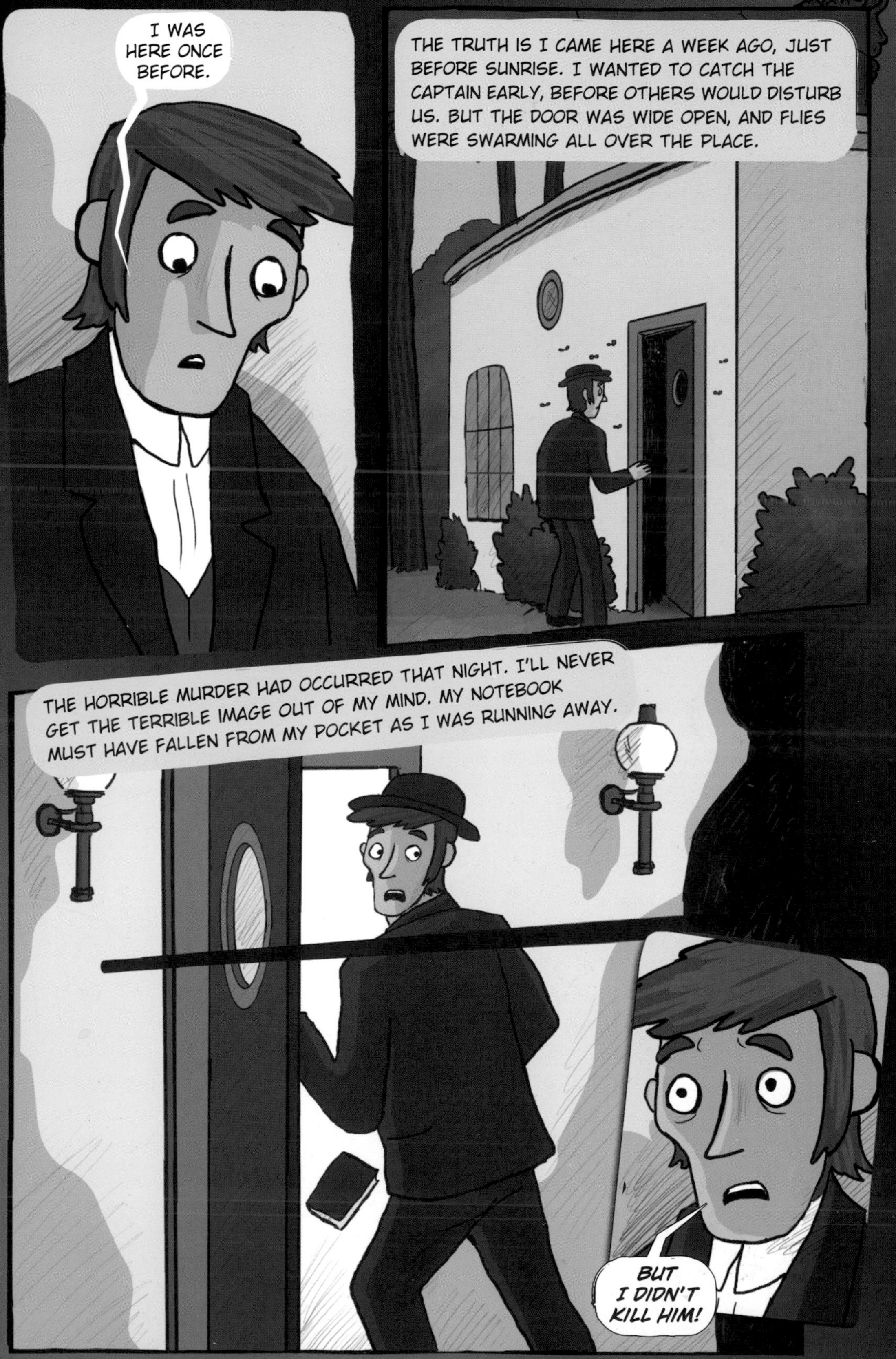
I WAS HERE ONCE BEFORE.
THE TRUTH IS I CAME HERE A WEEK AGO, JUST BEFORE SUNRISE. I WANTED TO CATCH THE CAPTAIN EARLY, BEFORE OTHERS WOULD DISTURB US. BUT THE DOOR WAS WIDE OPEN, AND FLIES WERE SWARMING ALL OVER THE PLACE.
THE HORRIBLE MURDER HAD OCCURRED THAT NIGHT. I'LL NEVER GET THE TERRIBLE IMAGE OUT OF MY MIND. MY NOTEBOOK MUST HAVE FALLEN FROM MY POCKET AS I WAS RUNNING AWAY.
BUT I DIDN'T KILL HIM!

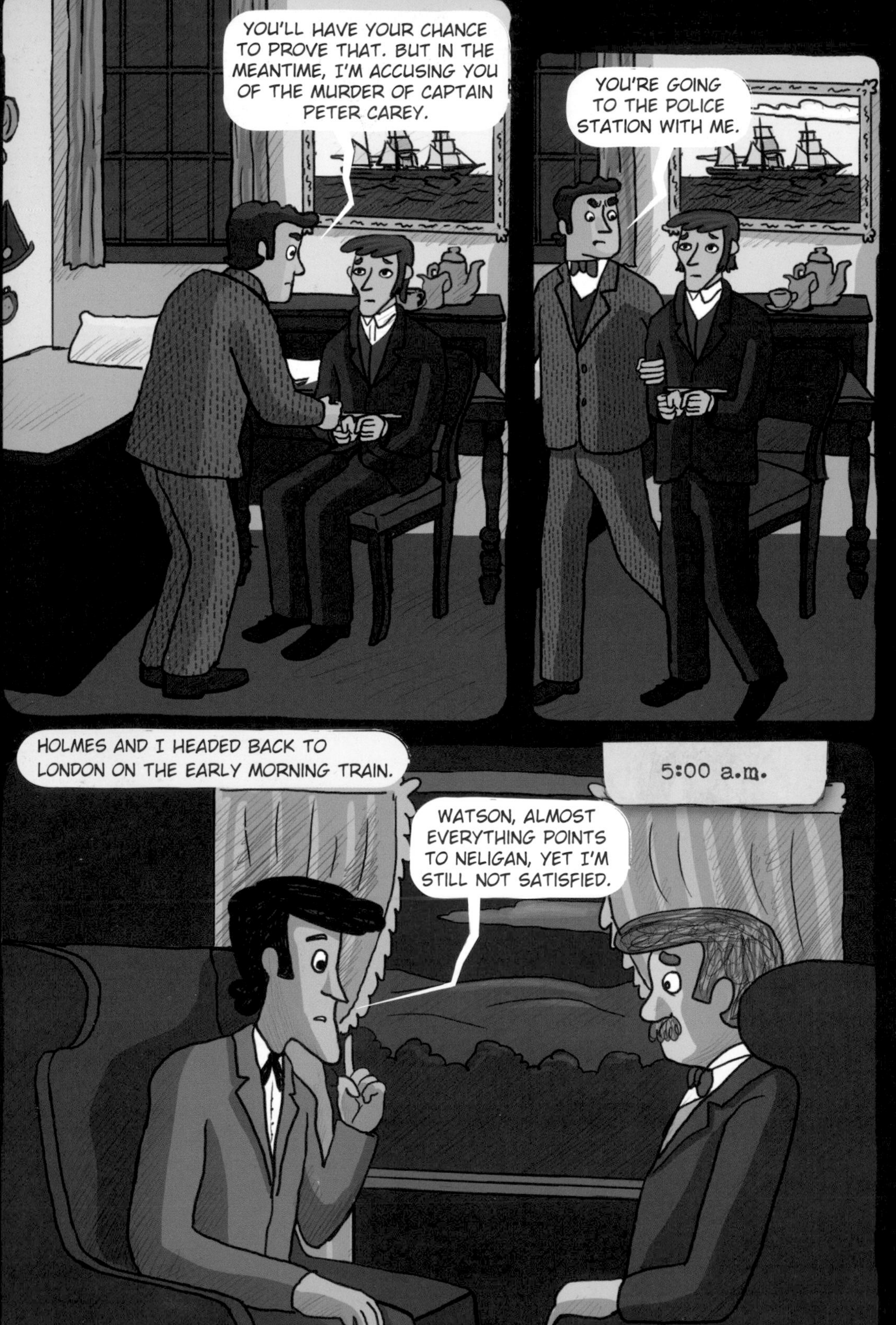
YOU'LL HAVE YOUR CHANCE TO PROVE THAT. BUT IN THE MEANTIME, I'M ACCUSING YOU OF THE MURDER OF CAPTAIN PETER CAREY.
YOU'RE GOING TO THE POLICE STATION WITH ME.
HOLMES AND I HEADED BACK TO LONDON ON THE EARLY MORNING TRAIN.
5:00 a.m.
WATSON, ALMOST EVERYTHING POINTS TO NELIGAN, YET I'M STILL NOT SATISFIED.

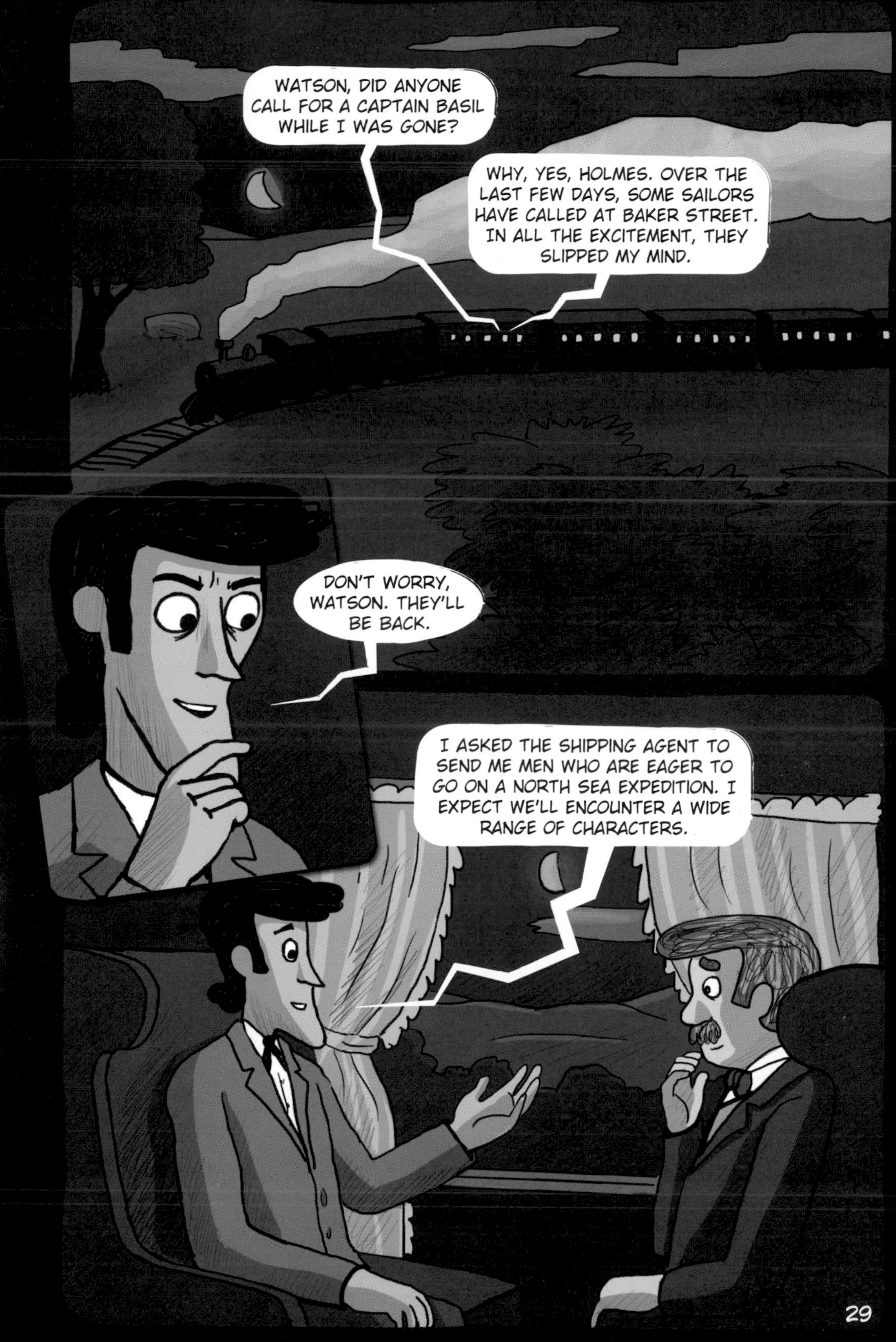
WATSON, DID ANYONE CALL FOR A CAPTAIN BASIL WHILE I WAS GONE?
WHY, YES, HOLMES. OVER THE LAST FEW DAYS, SOME SAILORS HAVE CALLED AT BAKER STREET. IN ALL THE EXCITEMENT, THEY SLIPPED MY MIND.
DON'T WORRY, WATSON. THEY'LL BE BACK.
I ASKED THE SHIPPING AGENT TO SEND ME MEN WHO ARE EAGER TO GO ON A NORTH SEA EXPEDITION. I EXPECT WE'LL ENCOUNTER A WIDE RANGE OF CHARACTERS.

I lay back in my seat and tried to sleep. I knew better than to question Holmes further. He wasn't going to tell me about his investigative methods until they had proven successful. So now I had one more mystery to ponder—why was Holmes playing the part of Captain Basil?

Early the next morning, two telegrams arrived for Holmes. He opened them eagerly and then broke into a quiet chuckle of satisfaction. He told me briefly of their contents. One was a list of names from a whaling company in Scotland. The other was a brief message from the shipping agent, listing the sailors who would visit Captain Basil the next morning.

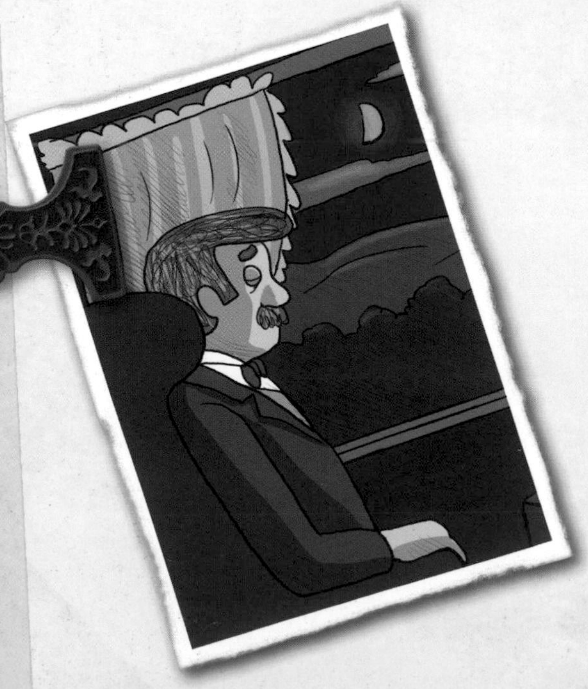

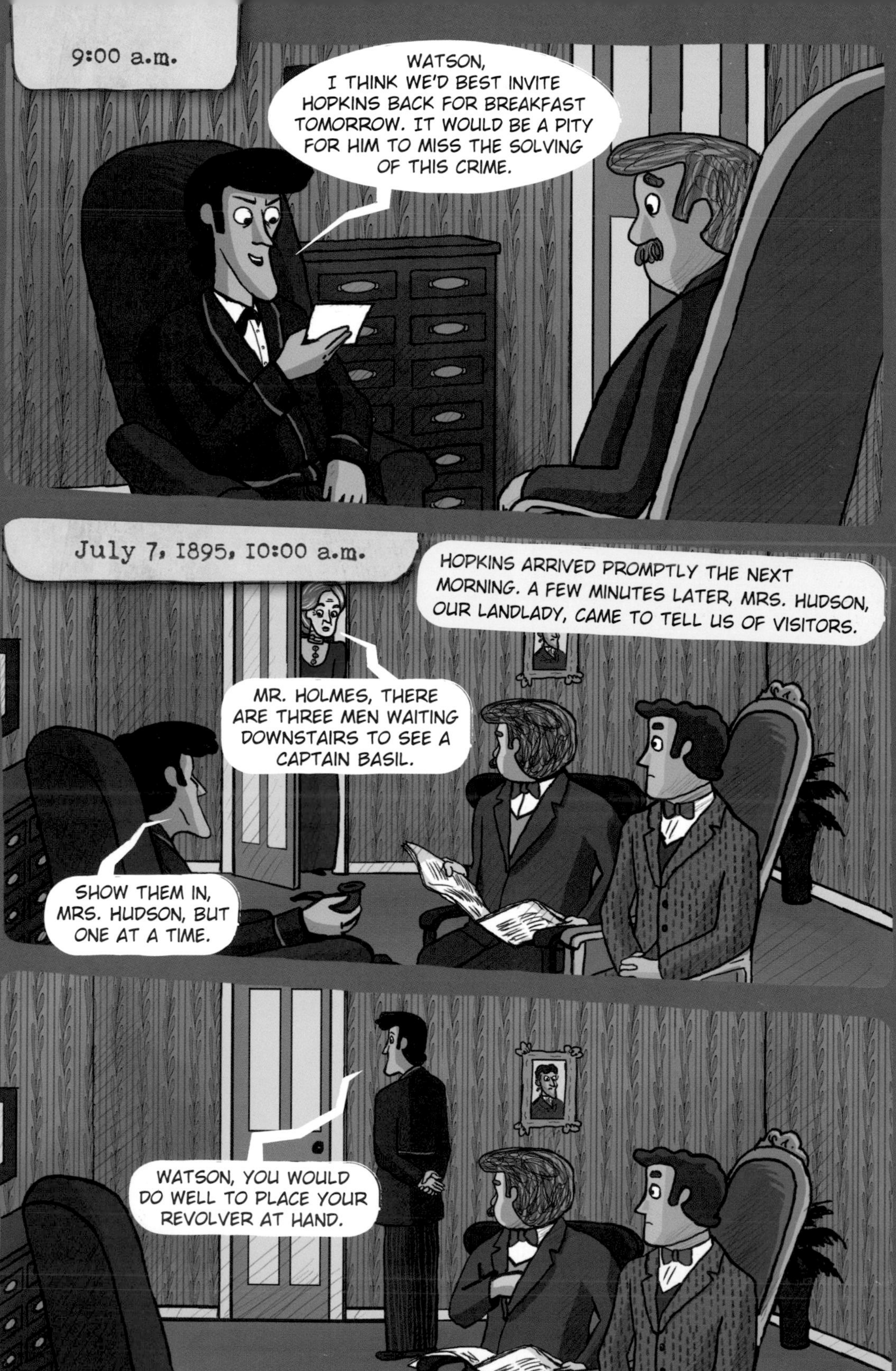
9:00 a.m.
WATSON, I THINK WE'D BEST INVITE HOPKINS BACK FOR BREAKFAST TOMORROW. IT WOULD BE A PITY FOR HIM TO MISS THE SOLVING OF THIS CRIME.
July 7, 1895, 10:00 a.m.
HOPKINS ARRIVED PROMPTLY THE NEXT MORNING. A FEW MINUTES LATER, MRS. HUDSON, OUR LANDLADY, CAME TO TELL US OF VISITORS.
MR. HOLMES, THERE ARE THREE MEN WAITING DOWNSTAIRS TO SEE A CAPTAIN BASIL.
SHOW THEM IN, MRS. HUDSON, BUT ONE AT A TIME.
WATSON, YOU WOULD DO WELL TO PLACE YOUR REVOLVER AT HAND.

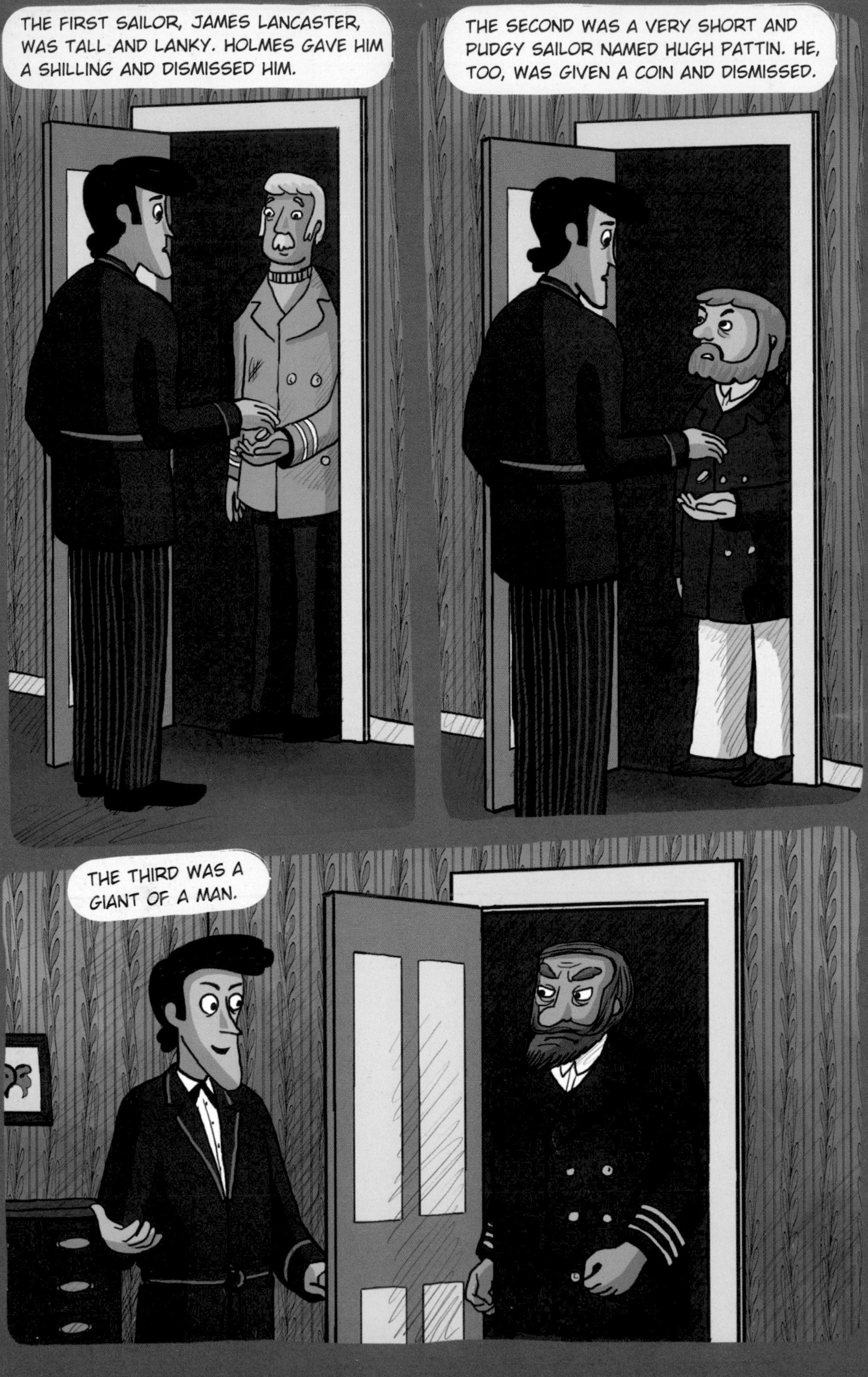
THE FIRST SAILOR, JAMES LANCASTER, WAS TALL AND LANKY. HOLMES GAVE HIM A SHILLING AND DISMISSED HIM.
THE SECOND WAS A VERY SHORT AND PUDGY SAILOR NAMED HUGH PATTIN. HE, TOO, WAS GIVEN A COIN AND DISMISSED.
THE THIRD WAS A GIANT OF A MAN.

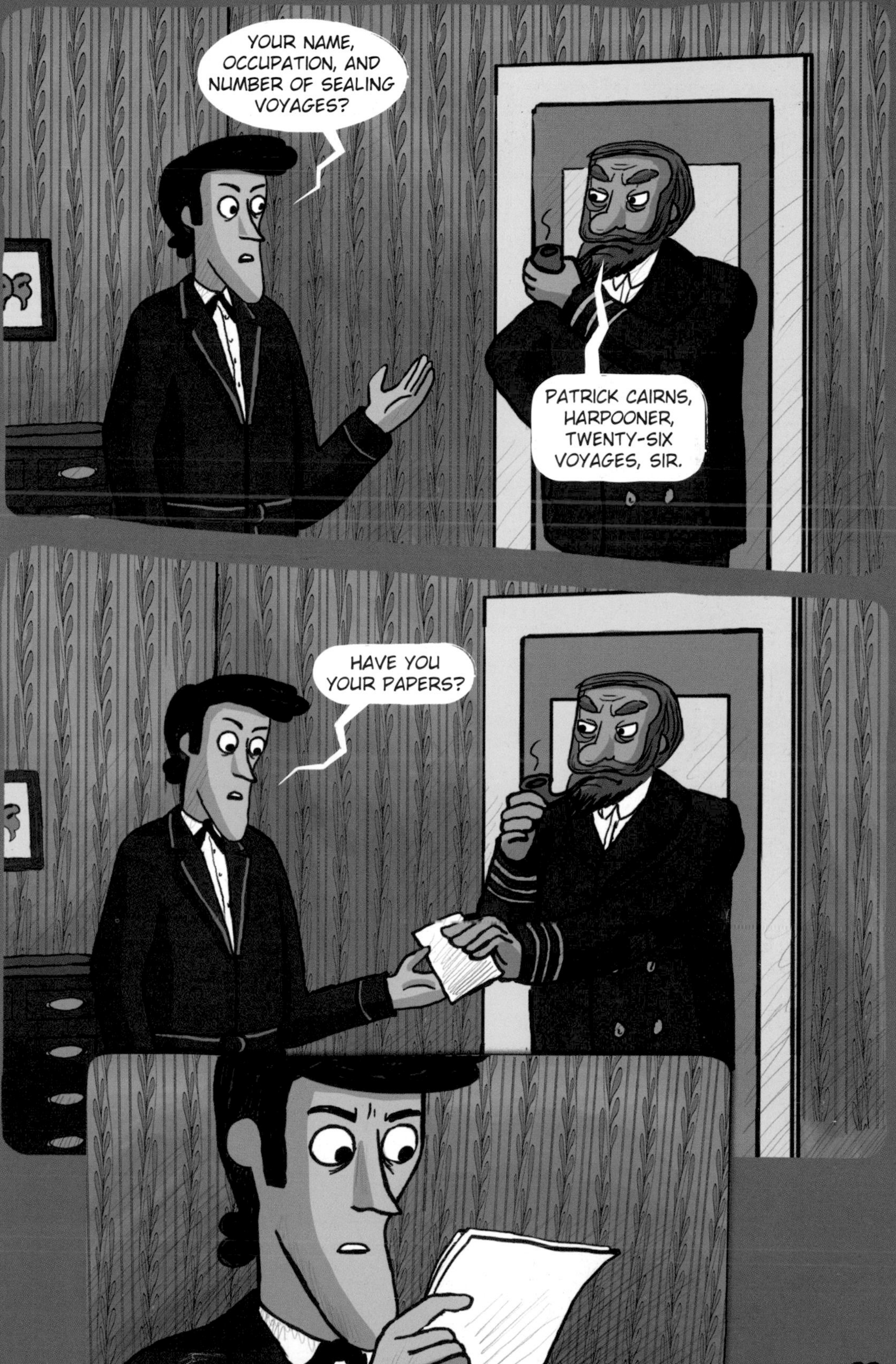
YOUR NAME, OCCUPATION, AND NUMBER OF SEALING VOYAGES?
PATRICK CAIRNS, HARPOONER, TWENTY-SIX VOYAGES, SIR.
HAVE YOU YOUR PAPERS?

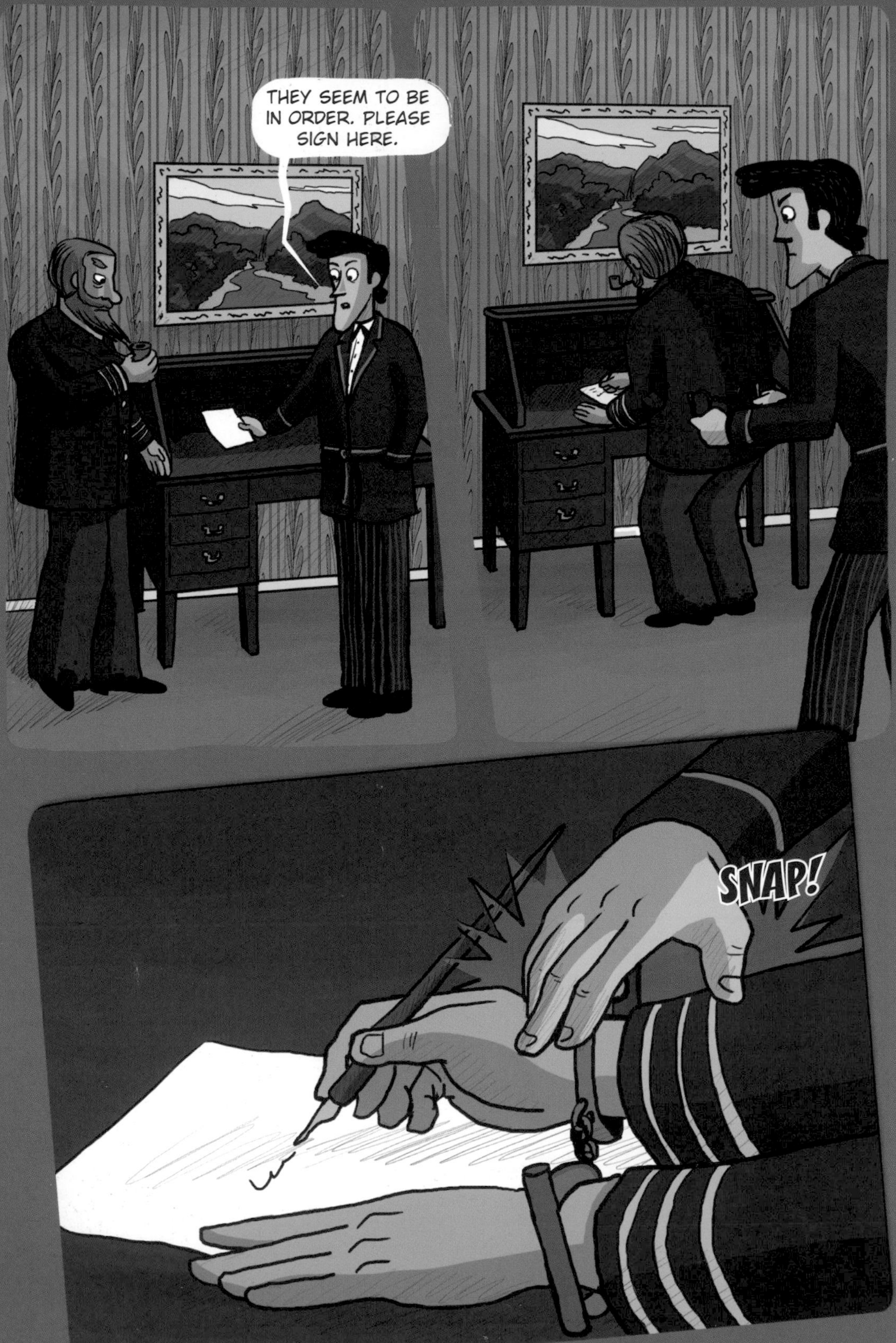
THEY SEEM TO BE IN ORDER. PLEASE SIGN HERE.
SNAP!

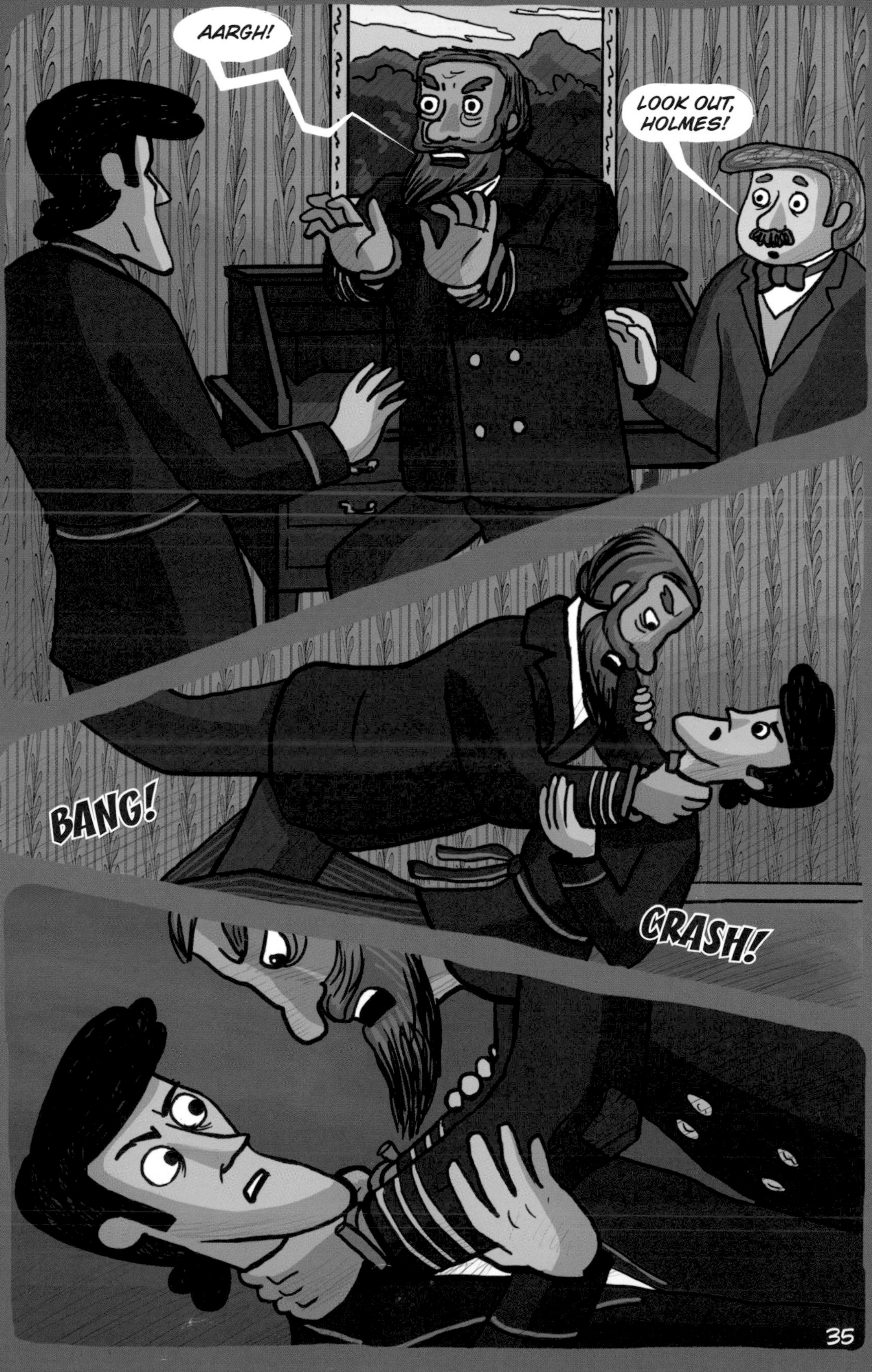
AARGH!
LOOK OUT, HOLMES!
BANG!
CRASH!

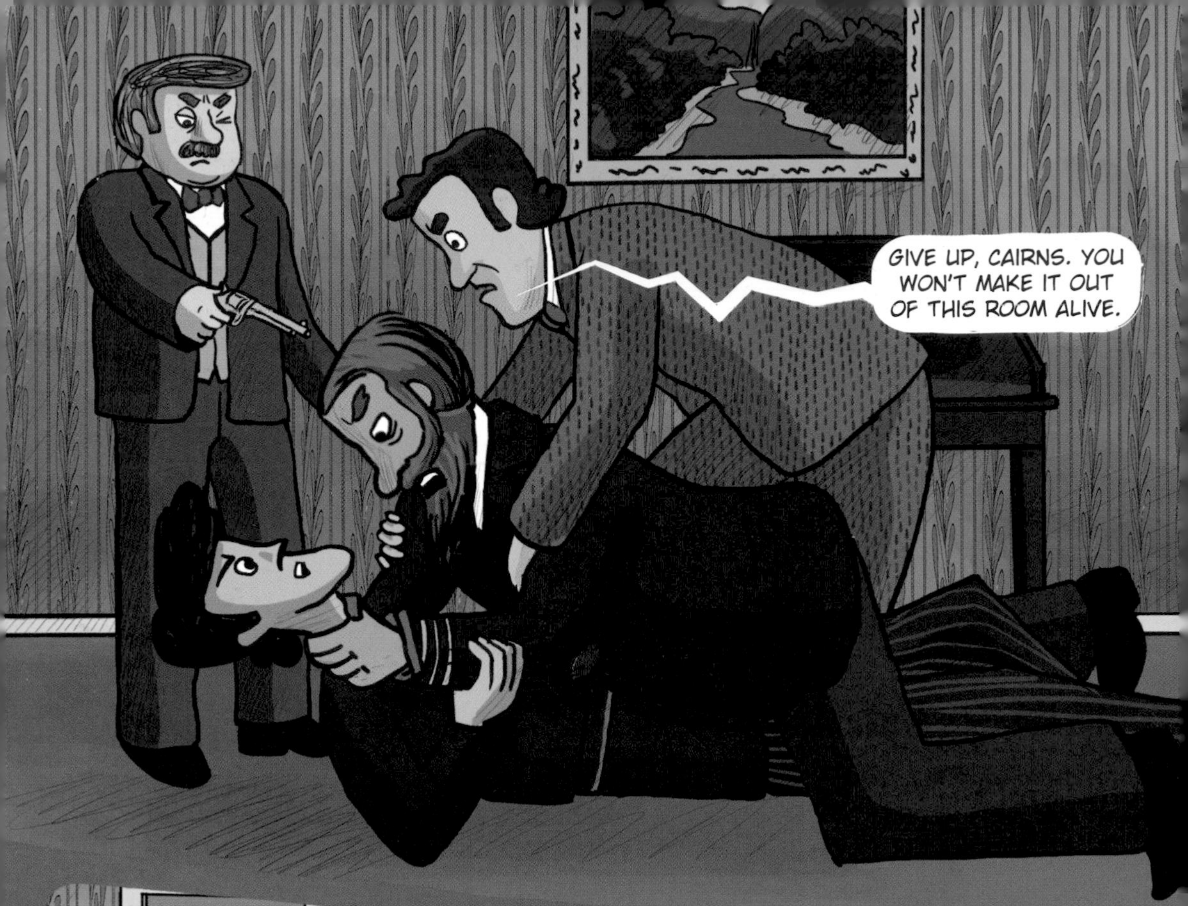
GIVE UP, CAIRNS. YOU WON'T MAKE IT OUT OF THIS ROOM ALIVE.

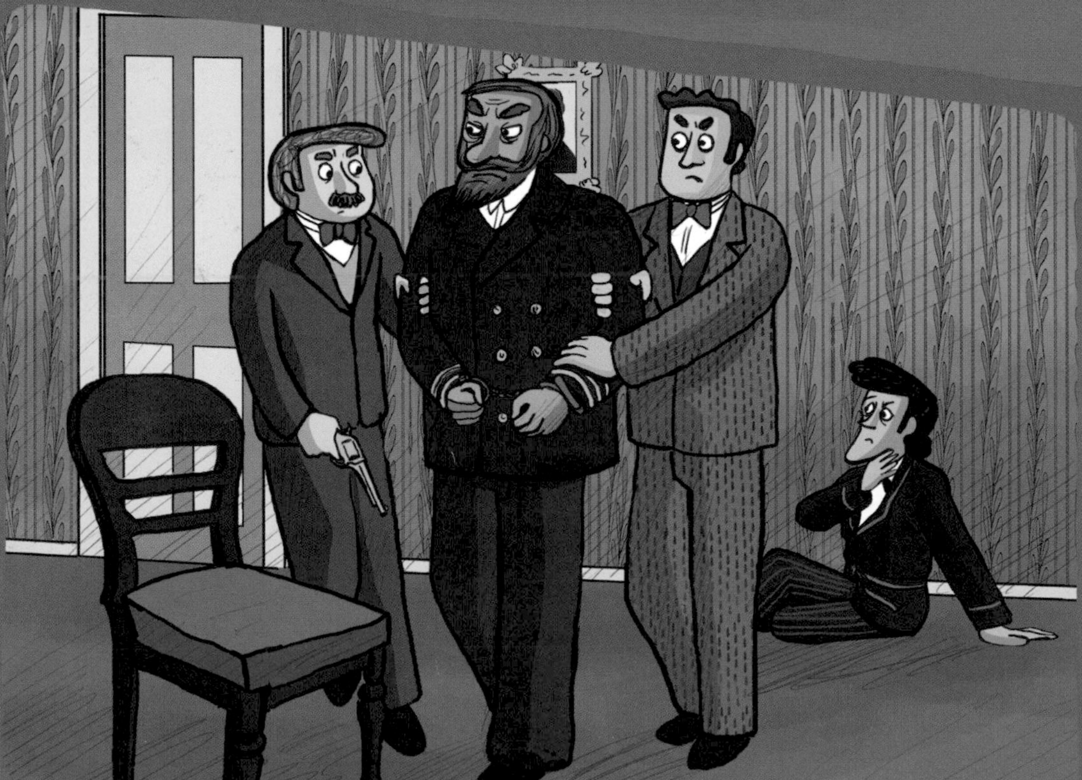

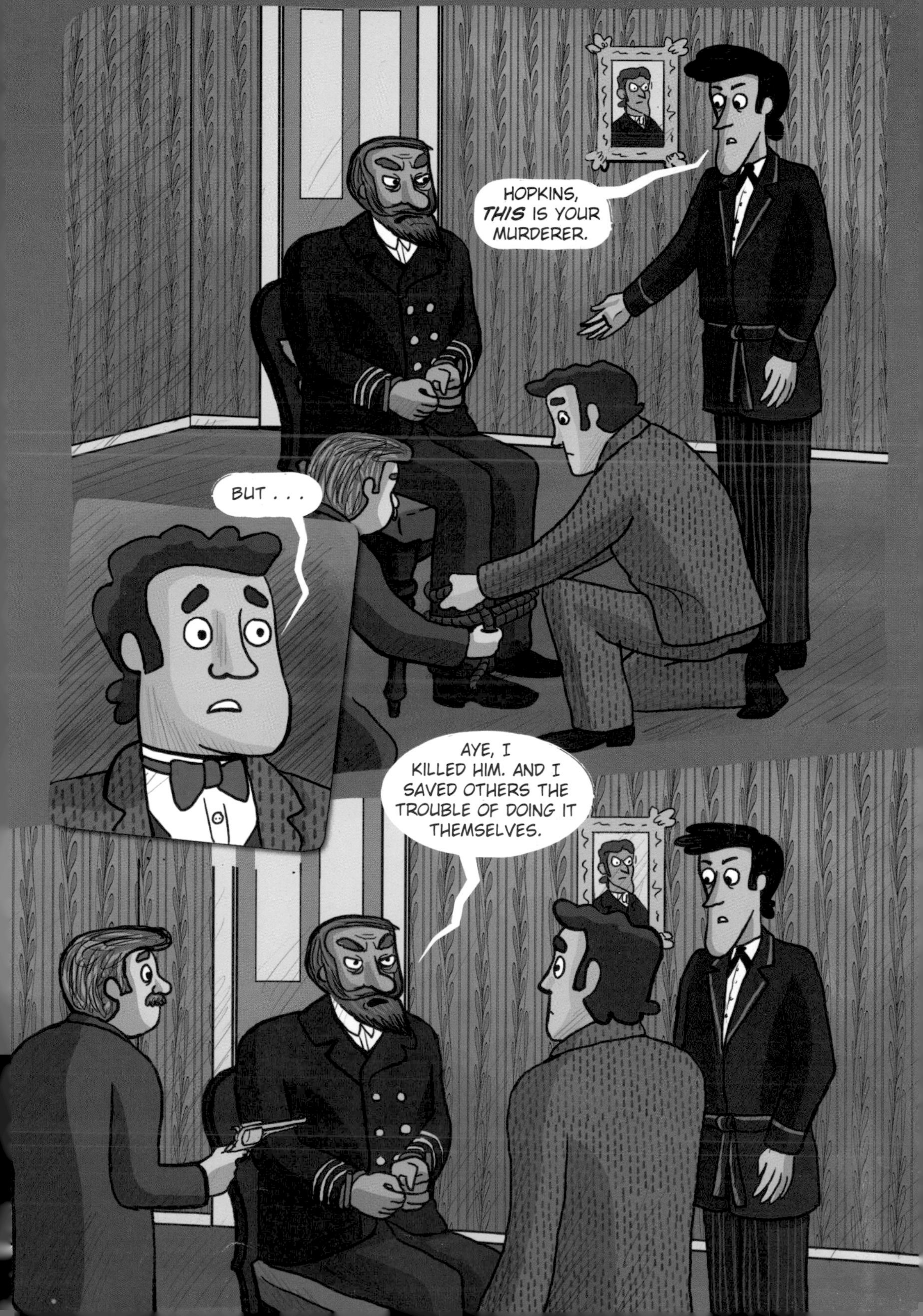
HOPKINS, *THIS* IS YOUR MURDERER.
BUT . . .
AYE, I KILLED HIM. AND I SAVED OTHERS THE TROUBLE OF DOING IT THEMSELVES.

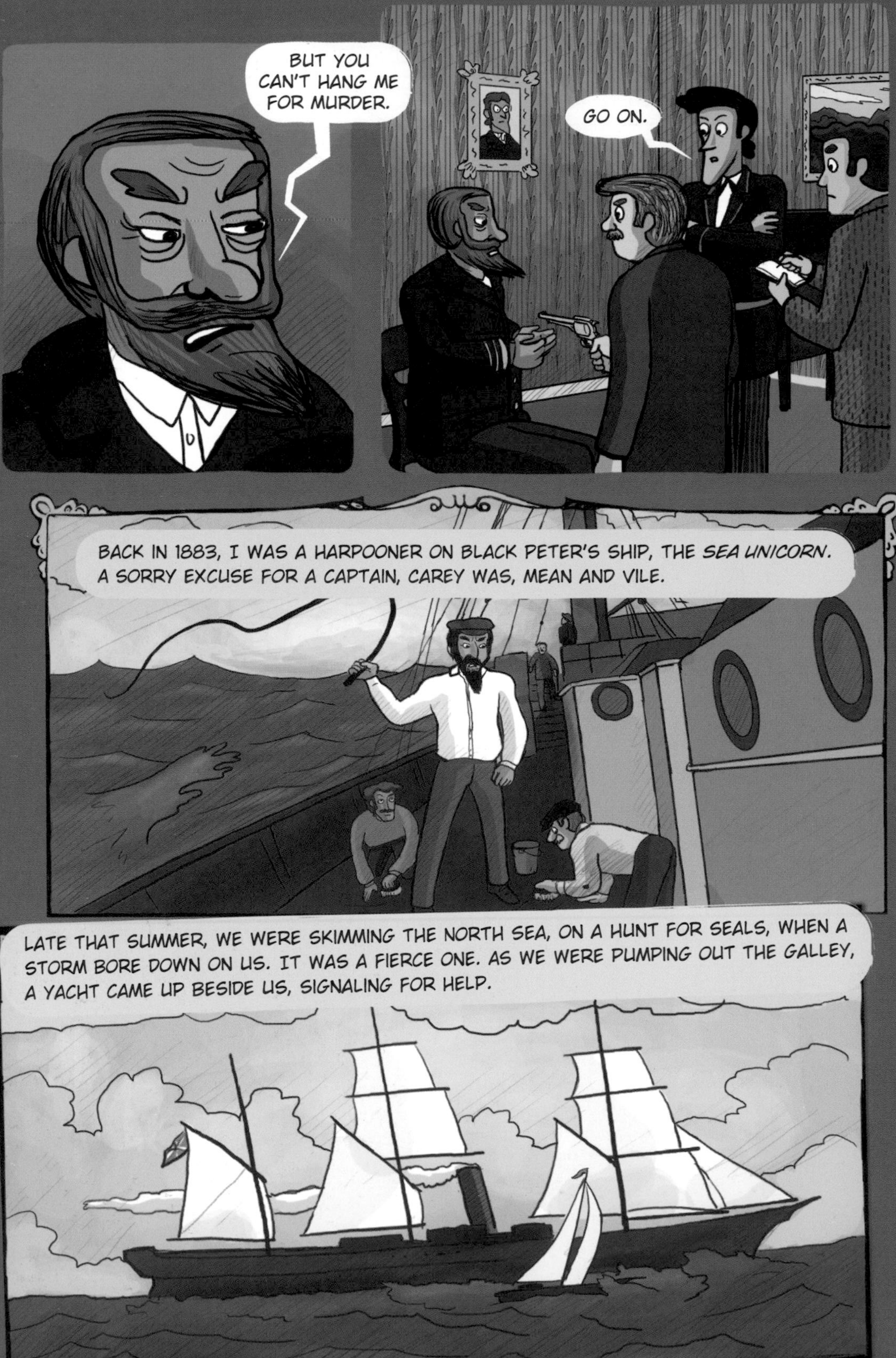
BUT YOU CAN'T HANG ME FOR MURDER.
GO ON.
BACK IN 1883, I WAS A HARPOONER ON BLACK PETER'S SHIP, THE *SEA UNICORN*. A SORRY EXCUSE FOR A CAPTAIN, CAREY WAS, MEAN AND VILE.
LATE THAT SUMMER, WE WERE SKIMMING THE NORTH SEA, ON A HUNT FOR SEALS, WHEN A STORM BORE DOWN ON US. IT WAS A FIERCE ONE. AS WE WERE PUMPING OUT THE GALLEY, A YACHT CAME UP BESIDE US, SIGNALING FOR HELP.

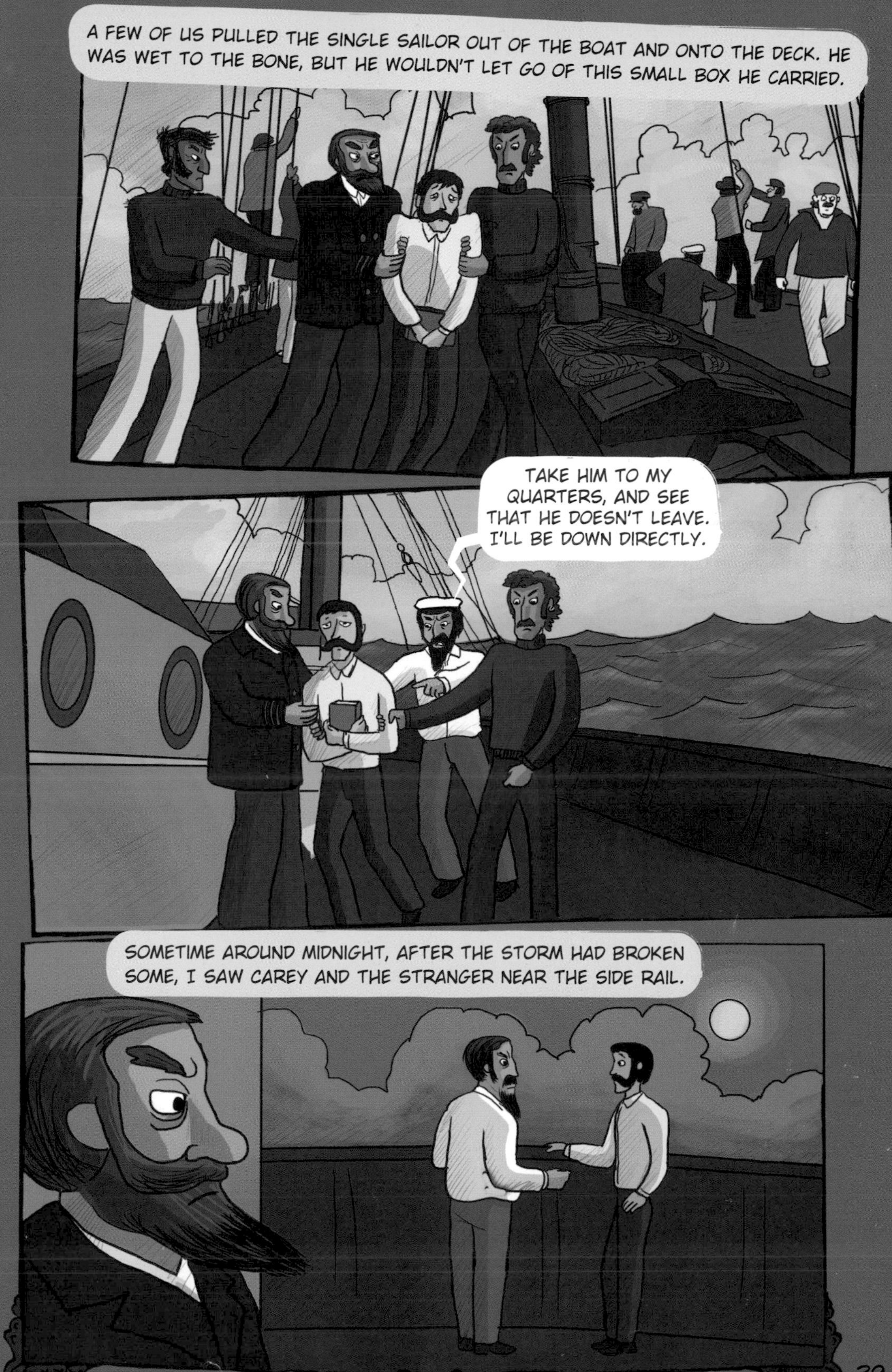
A FEW OF US PULLED THE SINGLE SAILOR OUT OF THE BOAT AND ONTO THE DECK. HE WAS WET TO THE BONE, BUT HE WOULDN'T LET GO OF THIS SMALL BOX HE CARRIED.
TAKE HIM TO MY QUARTERS, AND SEE THAT HE DOESN'T LEAVE. I'LL BE DOWN DIRECTLY.
SOMETIME AROUND MIDNIGHT, AFTER THE STORM HAD BROKEN SOME, I SAW CAREY AND THE STRANGER NEAR THE SIDE RAIL.

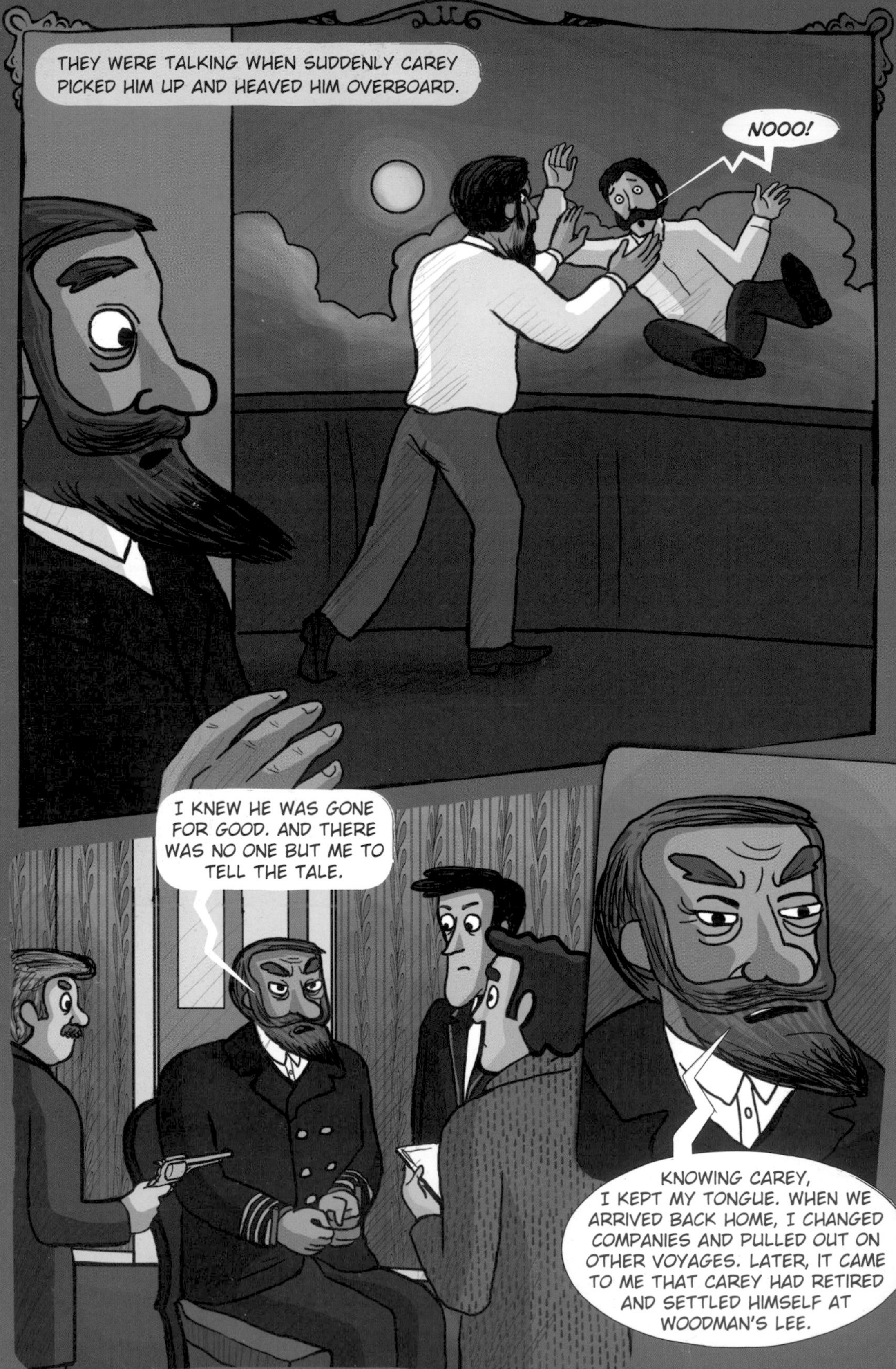

THEY WERE TALKING WHEN SUDDENLY CAREY PICKED HIM UP AND HEAVED HIM OVERBOARD.
NOOO!
I KNEW HE WAS GONE FOR GOOD. AND THERE WAS NO ONE BUT ME TO TELL THE TALE.
KNOWING CAREY, I KEPT MY TONGUE. WHEN WE ARRIVED BACK HOME, I CHANGED COMPANIES AND PULLED OUT ON OTHER VOYAGES. LATER, IT CAME TO ME THAT CAREY HAD RETIRED AND SETTLED HIMSELF AT WOODMAN'S LEE.

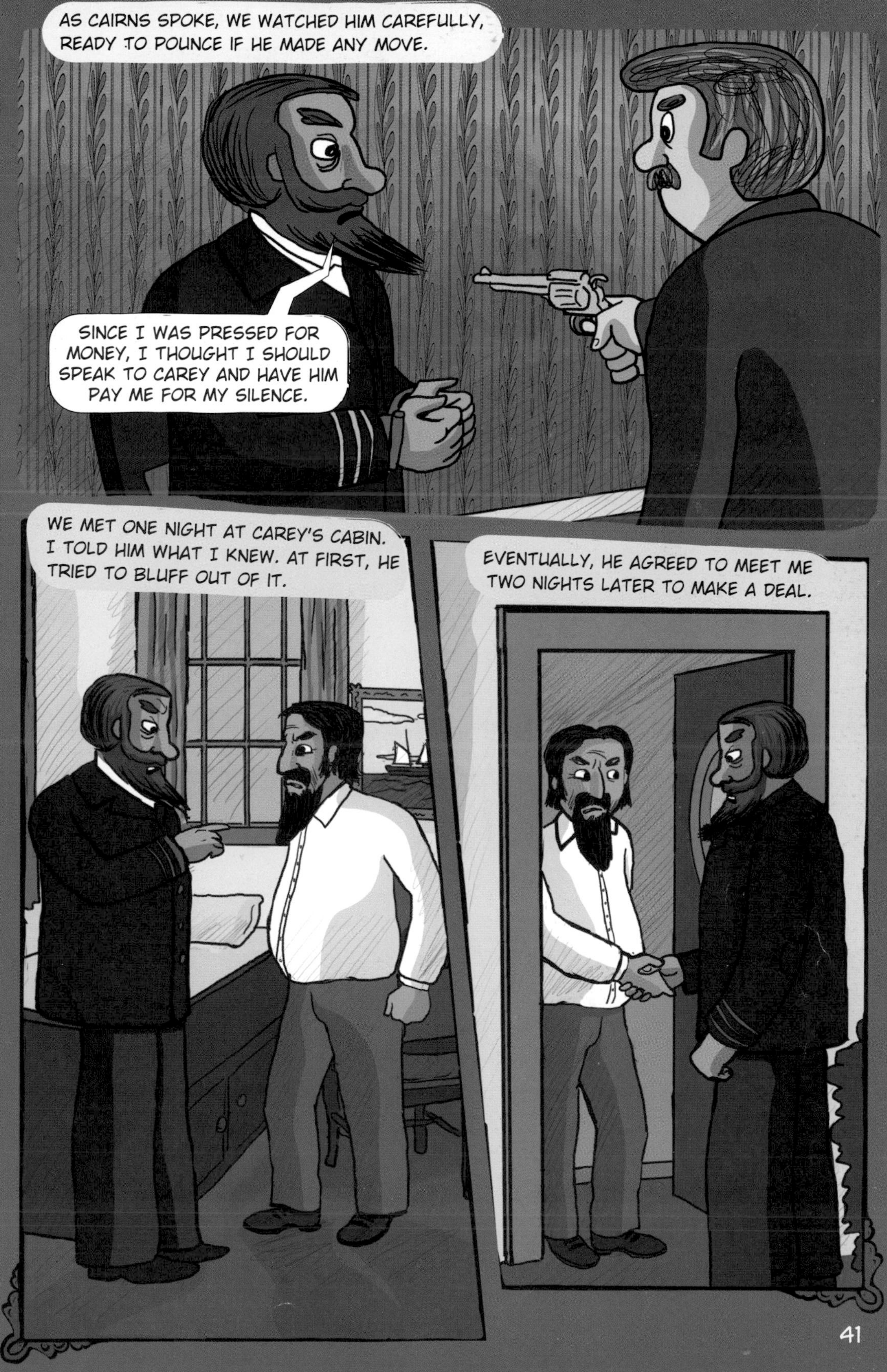
AS CAIRNS SPOKE, WE WATCHED HIM CAREFULLY, READY TO POUNCE IF HE MADE ANY MOVE.
SINCE I WAS PRESSED FOR MONEY, I THOUGHT I SHOULD SPEAK TO CAREY AND HAVE HIM PAY ME FOR MY SILENCE.
WE MET ONE NIGHT AT CAREY'S CABIN. I TOLD HIM WHAT I KNEW. AT FIRST, HE TRIED TO BLUFF OUT OF IT.
EVENTUALLY, HE AGREED TO MEET ME TWO NIGHTS LATER TO MAKE A DEAL.

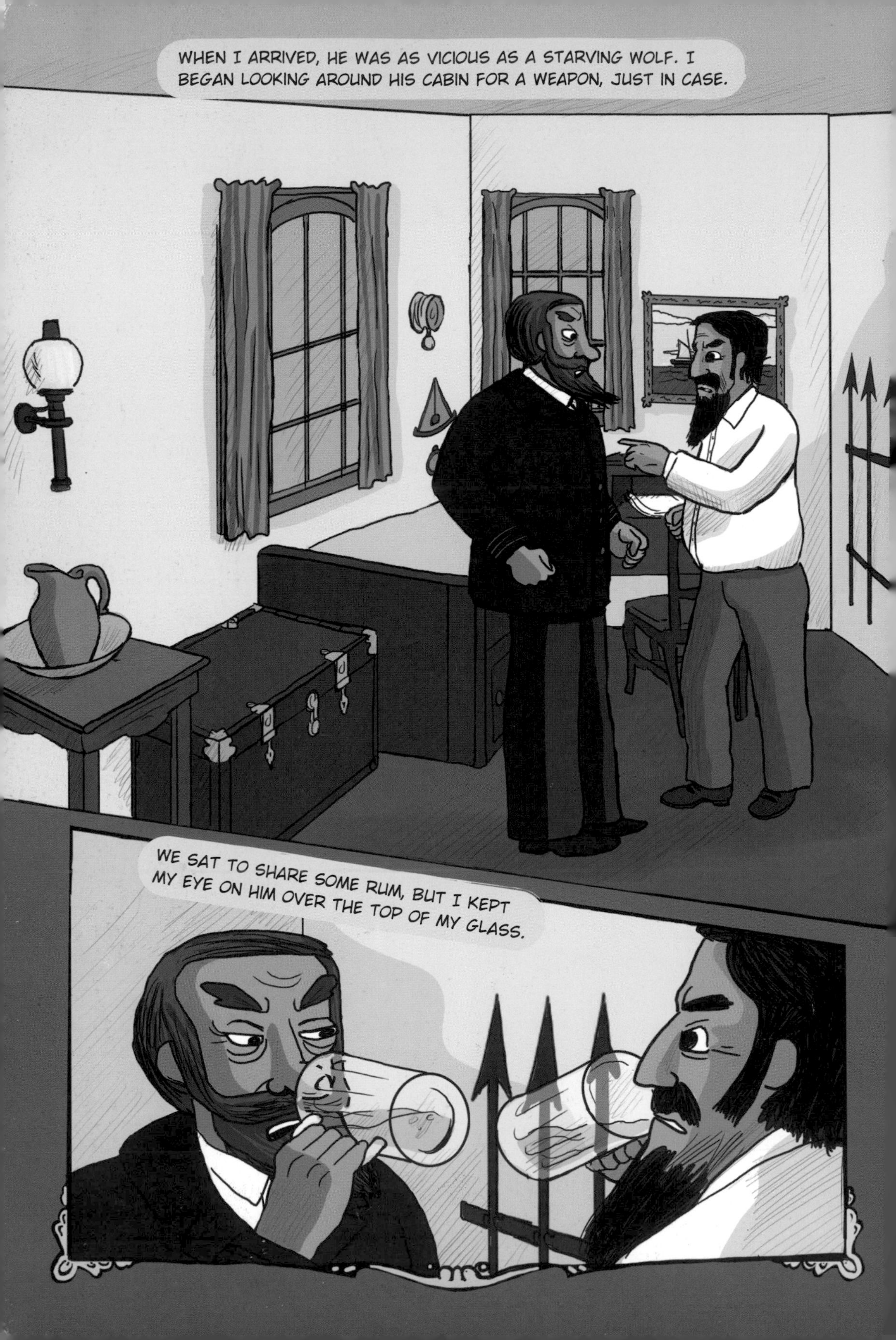
WHEN I ARRIVED, HE WAS AS VICIOUS AS A STARVING WOLF. I BEGAN LOOKING AROUND HIS CABIN FOR A WEAPON, JUST IN CASE.
WE SAT TO SHARE SOME RUM, BUT I KEPT MY EYE ON HIM OVER THE TOP OF MY GLASS.

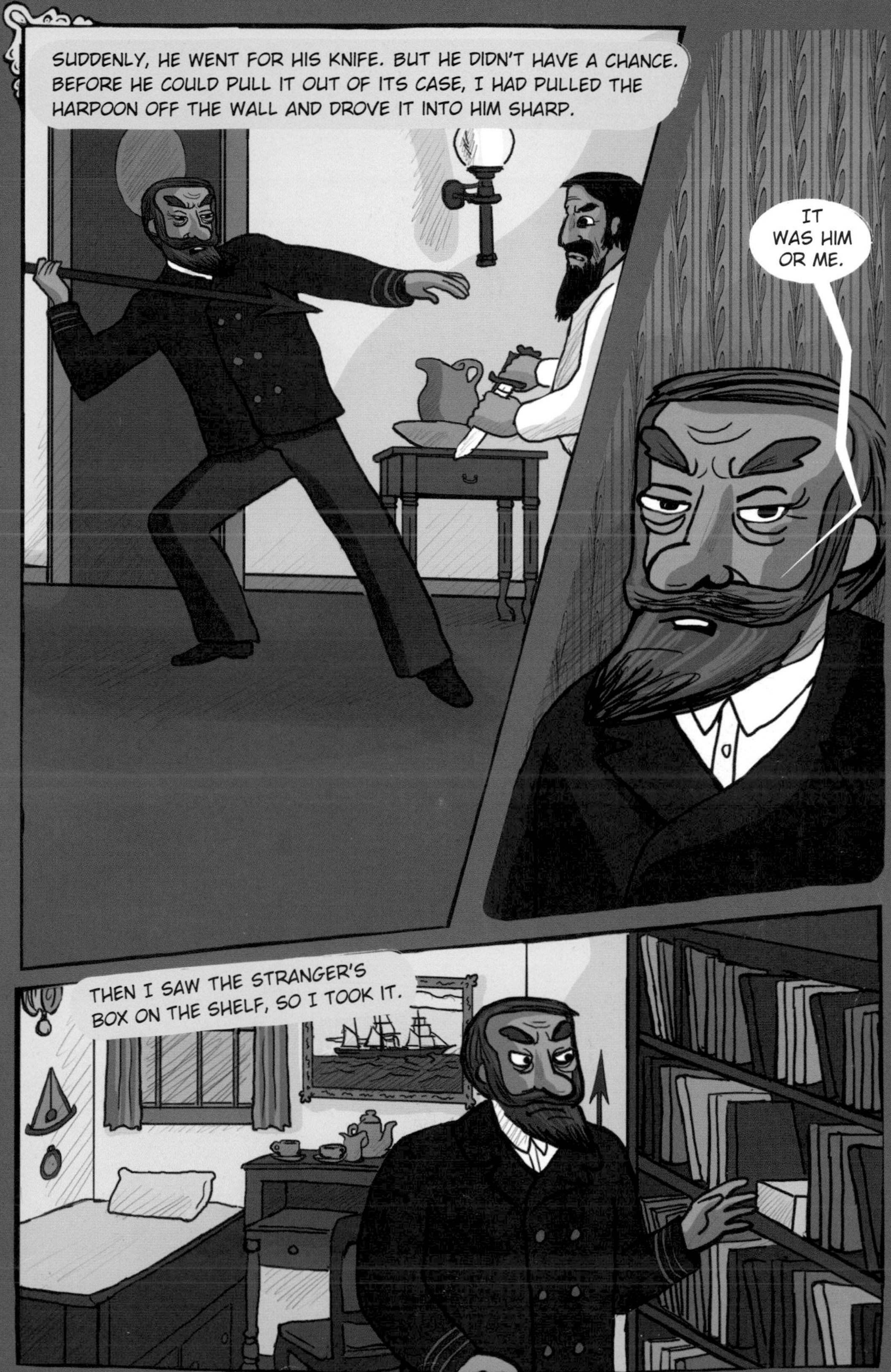
SUDDENLY, HE WENT FOR HIS KNIFE. BUT HE DIDN'T HAVE A CHANCE. BEFORE HE COULD PULL IT OUT OF ITS CASE, I HAD PULLED THE HARPOON OFF THE WALL AND DROVE IT INTO HIM SHARP.
IT WAS HIM OR ME.
THEN I SAW THE STRANGER'S BOX ON THE SHELF, SO I TOOK IT.

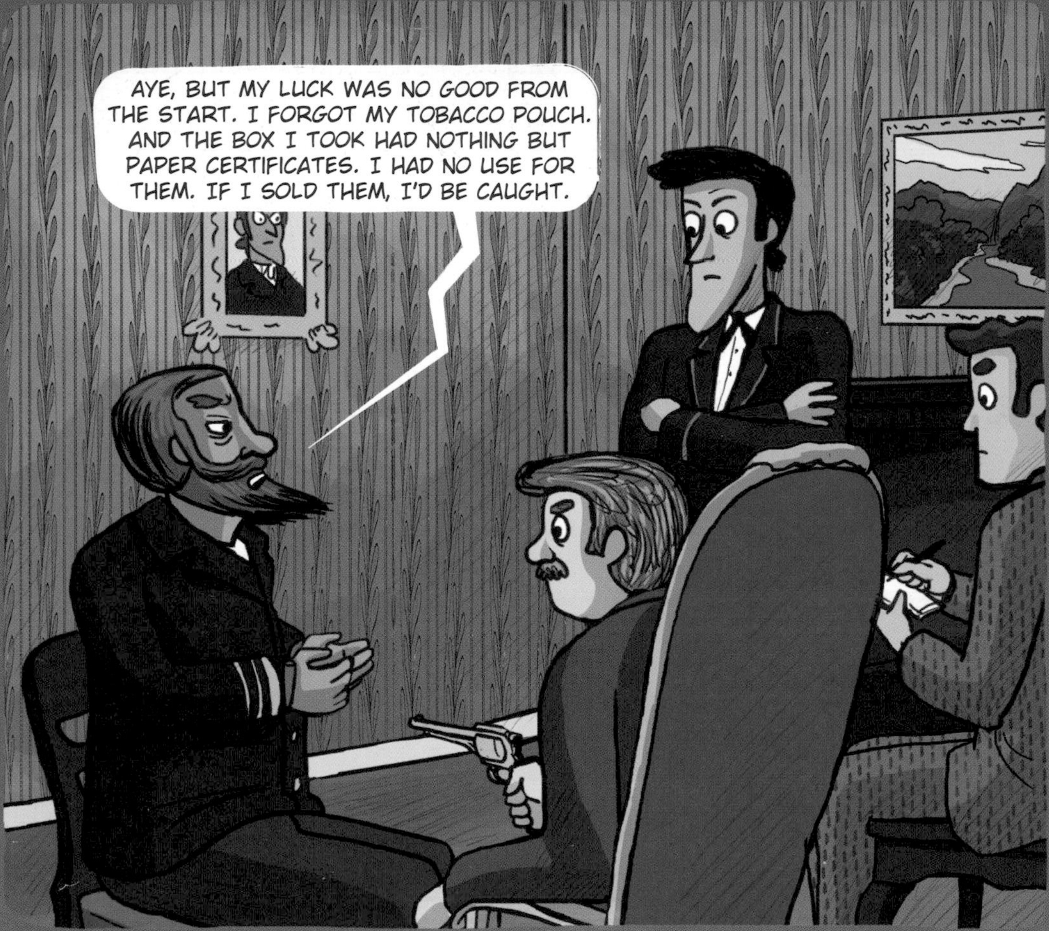
AYE, BUT MY LUCK WAS NO GOOD FROM THE START. I FORGOT MY TOBACCO POUCH. AND THE BOX I TOOK HAD NOTHING BUT PAPER CERTIFICATES. I HAD NO USE FOR THEM. IF I SOLD THEM, I'D BE CAUGHT.

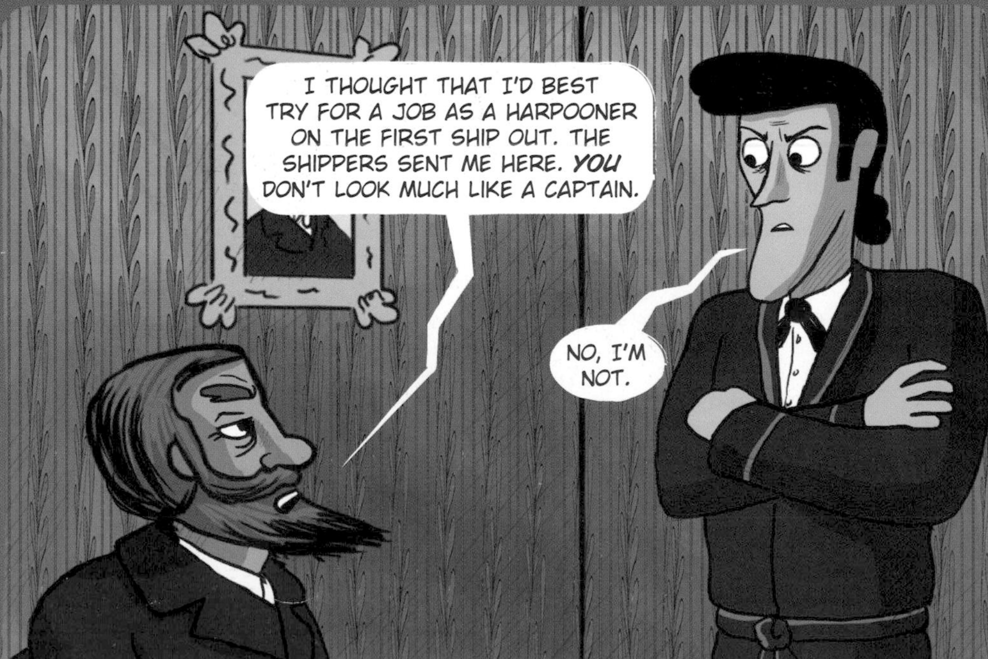
I THOUGHT THAT I'D BEST TRY FOR A JOB AS A HARPOONER ON THE FIRST SHIP OUT. THE SHIPPERS SENT ME HERE. ***YOU*** DON'T LOOK MUCH LIKE A CAPTAIN.
NO, I'M NOT.

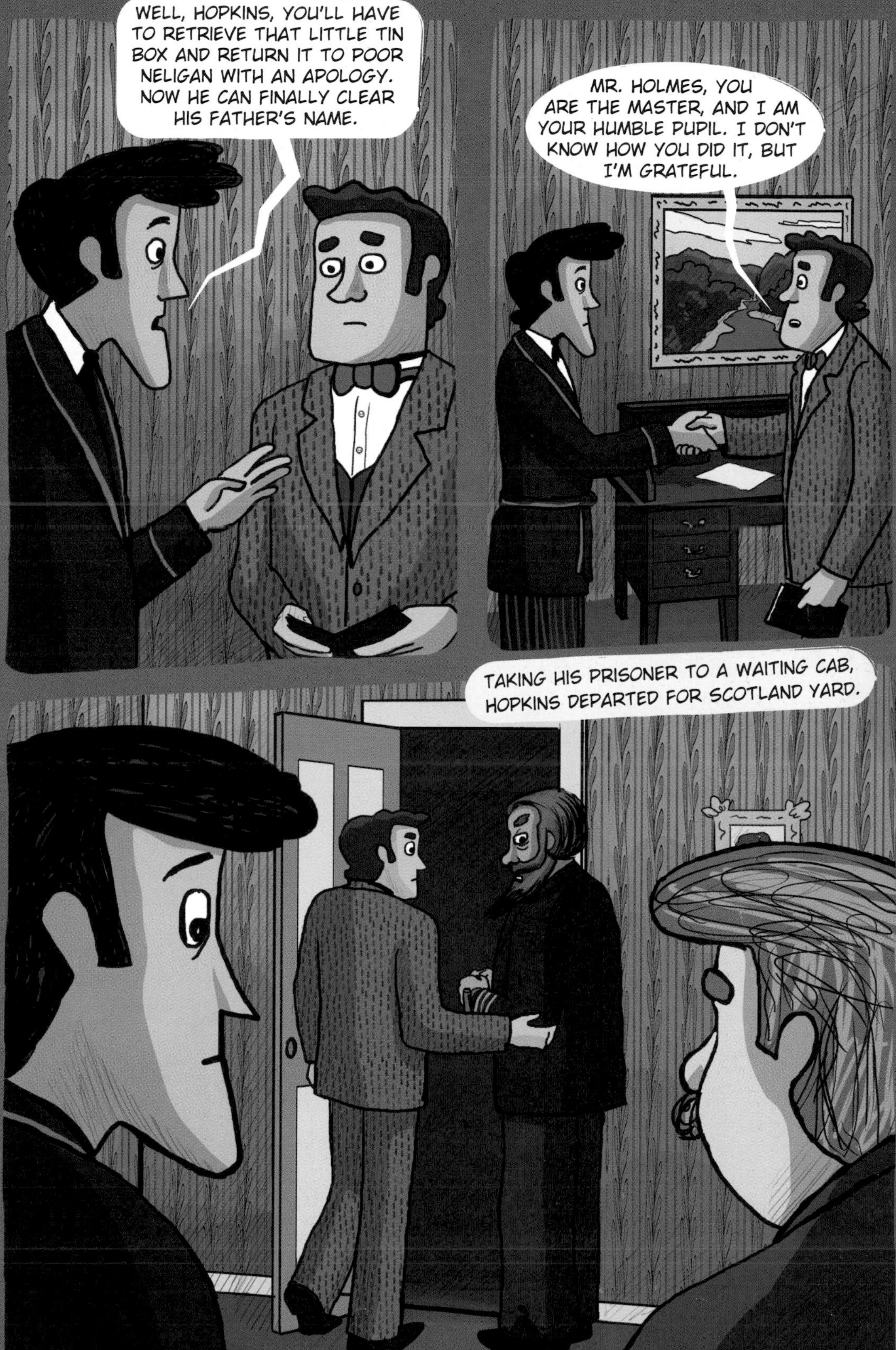
WELL, HOPKINS, YOU'LL HAVE TO RETRIEVE THAT LITTLE TIN BOX AND RETURN IT TO POOR NELIGAN WITH AN APOLOGY. NOW HE CAN FINALLY CLEAR HIS FATHER'S NAME.
MR. HOLMES, YOU ARE THE MASTER, AND I AM YOUR HUMBLE PUPIL. I DON'T KNOW HOW YOU DID IT, BUT I'M GRATEFUL.
TAKING HIS PRISONER TO A WAITING CAB, HOPKINS DEPARTED FOR SCOTLAND YARD.

From the Desk of
John H. Watson, M.D.

The Adventure of Black Peter: How Did Holmes Solve It?

How did Holmes know that Neligan did not kill Carey?

After reading about Carey's unusual murder, Holmes reasoned that the killer had to be powerful and skilled with a harpoon. To prove it, Holmes practiced on a dead pig. No matter how hard he tried, he couldn't drive a spear through the pig with one blow. When he met Neligan, he concluded that Neligan was not strong enough or experienced enough to have killed Carey.

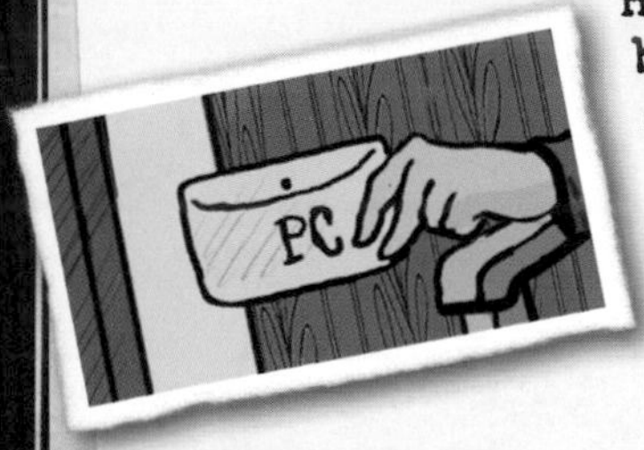
PC

How did Holmes know that the tobacco pouch belonged to Carey's killer?

The sealskin pouch had the initials P.C. printed on it. But Holmes did not assume that it belonged to the captain. Since a pipe was not found in the cabin, Holmes suspected that the pouch could belong to the unidentified killer.

How did Holmes figure out that Cairns was Carey's killer?

Carey was only a captain for a short time. Holmes suspected that there was an unusual reason for Carey's early retirement. Therefore, he was curious about Carey's life on the ship just before his retirement. Since harpooners work on whaling and sealing ships, Holmes figured that the killer was probably a harpooner on the *Sea Unicorn*. So he wired the company in Scotland for the ship's 1883 crew roster. This list of names came in one of the telegrams. Holmes looked down the list and found a harpooner with the initials P.C.—Patrick Cairns.

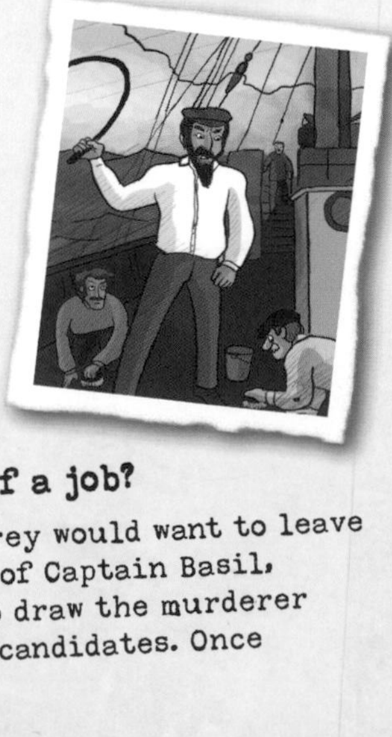

Why did Holmes suspect that the tin box was an important clue in the crime?

Neligan mentioned that his father's certificates had been kept in a small tin box. And it was known that Carey had had the certificates. For that reason, Holmes suspected the object removed from the logbook shelf was the tin box.

How did Holmes know that he could lure Cairns to his apartment with the promise of a job?

Holmes reasoned that the harpooner who killed Carey would want to leave England as quickly as possible. So under the name of Captain Basil, Holmes offered high wages and a long sea voyage to draw the murderer out. The shipping company sent Holmes the likely candidates. Once Holmes met Cairns, he knew he had the right man.

Further Reading and Websites

Cook, Peter. *You Wouldn't Want to Sail on a 19th Century Whaling Ship!: Grisly Tasks You'd Rather Not Do.* New York: Children's Press, 2004.

Cosson, M. J. *Yankee Whalers.* New York: Rourke Publishing, 2007.

Currie, Stephen. *Thar She Blows: American Whaling in the Nineteenth Century.* Minneapolis: Twenty-First Century Books, 2001.

Kassirer, Sue. *Thar She Blows: Whaling in the 1860s.* Norwalk, CT: Soundprints, 1997.

Kittredge, Frances. *Neeluk: An Eskimo Boy in the Days of the Whaling Ships.* Portland, OR: Graphic Arts Center Publishing Company, 2003.

Melville, Herman. *Moby Dick: Or, the Whale.* New York: Simon & Schuster, 2001.

Melville, Herman. *Moby Dick: The Graphic Novel.* New York: Barron's Educational, 2007.

Sandler, Martin. *Trapped in Ice!: An Amazing True Whaling Adventure.* New York: Scholastic Press, 2006.

Sherlock Holmes Museum
http://www.sherlock-holmes.co.uk

Sir Arthur Conan Doyle Society
http://www.ash-tree.bc.ca/acdsocy.html

221 Baker Street
http://221bakerstreet.org

About the Author

Sir Arthur Conan Doyle was born on May 22, 1859. He became a doctor in 1882. When this career did not prove successful, Doyle started writing stories. In addition to the popular Sherlock Holmes short stories and novels, Doyle also wrote historical novels, romances, and plays.

About the Adapters

Murray Shaw's lifelong passion for Sherlock Holmes began when he was a child. He was the author of the Match Wits with Sherlock Holmes series published in the 1990s. For decades, he was a popular speaker in public schools and libraries on the adventures of Holmes and Watson.

M. J. Cosson is the author of more than fifty books, both fiction and nonfiction, for children and young adults. She has long been a fan of mysteries and especially of the great detective, Sherlock Holmes. In fact, she has participated in the production of several Sherlock Holmes plays. A native of Iowa, Cosson lives in the Texas Hill Country with her husband, dogs, and cat.

About the Illustrators

French artist Sophie Rohrbach began her career after graduating in display design at the Chambre des Commerce. She went on to design displays in many top department stores including Galerias Lafayette. She also studied illustration at Emile Cohl school in Lyon, France, where she now lives with her daughter. Rohrbach has illustrated many children's books. She is passionate about the colors and patterns that she uses in her illustrations.

JT Morrow has worked as a freelance illustrator for over twenty years and has won several awards. He specializes in doing parodies and imitations of the Old and Modern Masters—everyone from da Vinci to Picasso. JT also exhibits his paintings at galleries near his home. He lives just south of San Francisco with his wife and daughter.